I0620274

THE VIGILANTE'S LOVER

VOL. 1

Annie Winters
Tony West

www.anniewinters.com
www.tonywestwrites.com

casey shay press

This is a work of fiction. All the characters, organizations, and events portrayed in this novel are either products of the author's imagination or used fictitiously.

Casey Shay Press
PO Box 160116
Austin, TX 78716
www.caseyshaypress.com

ISBN: 9781938150340

Also available in digital format.
eISBN: 9781938150364

Library of Congress Control Number: 2014959995

FIRST EDITION

Also by Annie Winters

Writing as JJ Knight
The UNCAGED LOVE Series
The FIGHT FOR HER Series

Writing as Deanna Roy
Forever Innocent
Forever Loved
Forever Sheltered

Learn about appearances and events at
www.deannaroy.com

For Ian Fleming and his amazing 007
and for E.L. James who broke all the taboos

We stand on the shoulders of giants.

1

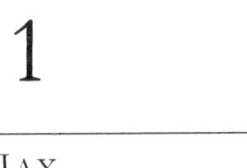

JAX

Ten minutes until the prison break.

I tilt my head, listening for a sign that my plan has been discovered. A change in the guard's pace. An alarm elsewhere in the compound. Unexpected voices or that particular sound of a hammer cocking in a gun.

But the normal routine is undisturbed.

If my team does the job well, it will remain that way, right up until I am gone.

Nine minutes.

I pass the time reading the last correspondence I sent to my extraction team regarding the escape. My own words reassure me that I have left nothing to chance.

The rope sizzles as it slides along your skin, like a flame zipping up a fuse. The stopper knot snaps into place, and you inhale sharply, ensnared by the bowline encircling your naked thigh.

Of course, there is no pretty girl on the receiving end. It isn't intended to be a love letter. It's the secret code I use with my network.

For those who understand it, I was clear in my instructions. Fire hazard. Prepare for a gas assault. Identify a secondary escape route.

I let no detail go unplanned.

Seven minutes.

The knots were my idea, an addition to our family code after my parents dropped out of the

Vigilante world. Ropes are elegant. Knots are useful. Everything about this language appeals to my sensibilities.

Beauty. Power. Bondage.

I enjoy all three.

A buzzer sounds at the end of the long hall. The new guard shift is coming on duty. There will be a five-minute changeover, then it's time to initiate the plan.

I'll be ready.

2

MIA

This big house is so quiet, and I have nothing to do. I can't help myself. I want to read the newest letter one more time.

I imagine sliding the corded rope through your silken folds. The first stopper knot catches against your swollen nub. You moan, and your voice is like a drug to my senses, intoxicating, addictive. I want to hear it again. I tug on the bowline, pushing the knot harder against your body.

My heart races dangerously fast. I press my hand against my chest as if that will slow it down.

I force my eyes from the page. If I don't stop reading now, I'll have another long lonely night on my cold pillow.

Actually, I will whether I keep reading it or not.

Your breathing speeds up and your hand reaches down. Naughty girl, I whisper, and loop a slipknot over your wrist. In a flash, your arm rises along the bedpost. I whip the rope around the wooden pole. You are secure now. At my mercy. Mine.

The paper crinkles in my trembling fingers. I flatten it back out on the wood surface of the old-fashioned desk that my aunt once prized more than any other item in her home. The house is so silent now that she is gone. Two weeks gone. Only the ticking of the grandfather clock in the front room breaks the eerie quiet.

I lean against the curved rails of the chair. Key parts of my body are warm and tense. I really should never have gotten involved in this crazy relationship, but it was just so…what had he called it?

Intoxicating. Addictive.

A long sigh escapes my chest. I pull the envelope from beneath the handwritten page and study the postmark for the hundredth time.

Ridley Prison.
Chicago, Illinois.

This is his latest reply. It arrived this morning, the only break in my long, strange days puttering around this empty house, unsure of what to do now that my last surviving family member has left me.

My finger traces the edges of the stamp. The postmark is a week ago. It took a while to arrive.

Probably someone in the prison had to read it and approve the contents. I wonder what they thought of it.

My eyes graze another line.

The stopper knot thrusts against you, eliciting another impassioned cry.

Must. Stop.

I stand up, fanning my face with the envelope. When the first letter turned up a few months ago, I assumed it was sent to the wrong address. Aunt Bea didn't seem the type to correspond with someone in prison.

But she was unable to speak by the time I arrived to help. The last stroke had been too much, stealing her speech and most of her motor functions. The neighbors who had been watching out for her could no longer manage, and she was about to be forced to live out her days in an eldercare facility twenty miles away. Our small Tennessee town has no nursing homes. Families are expected to take care of their own.

So I did. I dropped out of community college and moved back into the rambling old Victorian on the outskirts of town.

Of course, my arrival created a little rally in her health. Her happy eyes followed me whenever I came into her room to spoon her a little broth or adjust her pillows.

She had no way to communicate other than through hand squeezes and slight nods of her head. The letters weren't a priority in our limited conversations, which centered around hunger and comfort and big decisions about her house and accounts.

But now that she is gone, the letters are one of my few links to the outside world.

Of course the writer *would* have to be a prisoner. I glance at his name. I wonder if he is as sexy as he sounds.

Jax De Luca.

3

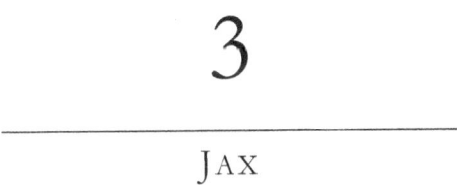

JAX

Five minutes to prison break.

I resist the urge to pace my cell. I'm at the mercy of two friends and comrades, Sam and Colette. I have only a meager handful of contacts I still trust.

We have a painfully short window to get me out of Ridley Prison before the other Vigilantes are alerted to my escape. I gave Sam and Colette every detail of the security and routine, picked up during the past year in this hellhole.

We're breaking out months ahead of schedule and without all the planning in place, but I feel I must. Something has happened to my closest comrade, Klaus. The letters coming from his safe house are garbled and out of code. This can only mean he has been compromised, captured, or worse.

Normally, breaking out of an ordinary prison is child's play. I've done it without assistance on more than one occasion. The difference this time is my fall from grace within the Vigilante network itself.

Work with them and anything is possible. Laws don't apply to you. Presidents and prime ministers answer your calls. You have no need to take theirs.

But cross the Vigilantes and you might as well be dead. Their reach is unsurpassed. They are part of every government, every agency, every group of mercenaries, every band of killers.

I know this well. I once was in line to become the head of it all.

Now they want me out of their way.

I pace in my cell and wait for the bell that signals the doors will open. I run through the plan again, over and over, until I can imagine every footfall. My mind's eye travels the halls and corridors, past suspicious guards with narrowed eyes and hands on weapons. It sees my fellow inmates, the nods of recognition and respect, the glowers of hate. Lots of enemies in here. I don't care. At least with adversaries, you know where you stand.

Unlike lovers. A lover is what got me here.

Jovana.

I shake my head. I can't get distracted now. Revenge will come when I'm out.

The alarm signaling the start of our workday echoes through the cell block. A second later my door rumbles open. I begin a mental countdown, honed to precision through years of training. Despite my preparation, I still have to force my breathing into a steady rhythm.

Relax, Jax.

It will do no good for the prison's mood measurement system to pick up any deviation from the norm. Even if the guards aren't monitoring it, the Vigilantes are. I recognize their tech over the pathetic measures the civilians put in place.

I step forward and glance up at the conduct screen on the wall outside my cell. Still green.

A disembodied voice barks a command from the speakers. "Inmates out and proceed to morning assignments."

My fellow prisoners shuffle out in a jumbled wave. Most stare straight ahead, their morning stimulants not yet kicking through their blood. These I ignore. They are of no consequence to my plan, aside from obstacles to sidestep, like one might avoid a pothole in the road.

A few cast glances at the others, though. Schemers, plotters, and the paranoid. They are the unknown element, something that could destroy all my hard work with an unexpected move.

I fall in with the flow of disenchanted humanity. Head forward, but aware of everyone around me. At the end of the cell block, the stream splits in two, then again at each intersection. Now we are only a few, but inmates from other cell blocks reinforce our numbers as we walk through the central hub.

I feel the unfriendly gaze of a guard fix on me. Johnson.

"De Luca! Step over here."

Johnson's voice holds a touch of malice. I move to stand in front of him, my expression neutral. He sneers as he looks me over, then waves a mood wand over my body. It hums a bluish green.

He frowns, seeming to expect something more interesting. He glances at my prison badge, which lists my morning assignment on a digital display.

"Book duty again? Figures an egg like yourself would land there as much as you can."

I say nothing. He loves to play these games, and I can little afford the time.

"No voice today, egg?" His mean eyes lock on mine. His face is unshaven in a way he probably assumes attracts women, but merely looks unkempt on his fat-cheeked jowls.

I cycle through words of calm in my head. "I have no say in my assignment," I answer with as little emotion as possible. His mood wand flickers.

Johnson laughs, a rough and unpleasant sound. In another place and a different time, I'd have floored him. I might yet. But for now I just wait.

"Like hell you don't," he says. "You're a schemer. And schemers work the system."

A vein throbs in his neck. His pulse is quickening, and I need to diffuse this now. He is acting out of the norm. The mood detection sensor will pick up on it, and my plan will unravel if we go into lockdown. The system doesn't care who is upset — inmate or guard. It just reacts.

"As you say, sir," I respond, my tone flat.

"Oh, I do," he says. "And I also say you ain't going to the library today. I got better plans for you."

My eyes drop to the wand in his hand. It flickers briefly into yellow. This isn't part of Johnson's game, though, so he flips it off and shoves it in his belt. The overhead monitors are much less sensitive.

"All right," I say, as if it doesn't matter to me either way. "But I believe McGruder provided the work assignments for today. He may feel differently."

Fat McGruder is the captain for my cell block. Evoking his name has the intended effect. Johnson exhales in anger through his nose.

For a moment I think he's going to grow a spine for once and go against his commander, but then he looks away.

"Get out of here, egg. Before I find an excuse to give you some physical reprimand."

"As you say, sir." The confrontation over, I don't make much effort to hide my amusement, but

Johnson doesn't seem to notice. Yes, I'll definitely come back to exact a bit of vengeance on this one.

I'm sixty seconds behind schedule. I quicken my pace to make up half that by the time I walk into the library, the least-patrolled room of the prison. I had to pull a lot of internal strings to get this duty. Traded a small fortune in cigarettes and low-tech weaponry. I took care to never arm anyone with something I couldn't defend against in my sleep. Didn't matter. They were grateful.

I scan my badge at the library entrance and head back into the stacks.

Rows of musty books line the gray metal shelves. They only reach up to my chest, a way to keep inmates in view. The guard glances my direction, a simple acknowledgment of my position, then turns back to his work.

"You're late," a deep voice whispers in my ear.

"I know," I say without turning. Sam is actually five rows away, but angled such that his voice projector can reach only me.

"*Little Women*," he says. "Third shelf."

I reach for the book and rub my thumb along the spine. I can feel the small form of the dart thrower underneath the material.

"Careful where you point that thing," Sam whispers.

I give him the barest nod, then walk back to the guard. Out of the corner of my eye I see Sam, dressed in the simple navy coveralls of a custodian, reposition himself. A click in my ear tells me he's rerouted the cameras in the room. I hold the book out to the guard, spine up. He looks at me, a question on his lips, and I press on the cover.

The man gives a small grunt of annoyance and reaches up to his neck. His eyes widen in surprise as his fingers brush the small bit of metal embedded in his skin. I can see the alarm in his expression, but it fades as the drug kicks in and he slumps to the side. I grab him before he can hit the floor and ease him down under the desk.

My fingers fly over his uniform. By the time Sam has joined me, I have the guard's shirt off. Sam already has his own coveralls unfastened, revealing a thin bag. I finish undressing the guard as Sam opens the bag and allows its contents to blossom forth. A pale gray suit. I shuck my prison orange, and Sam peels off his coveralls.

"You never cease to amaze, Sam." I finger the tailored suit. The fine cloth feels like heaven.

"Thank Colette for that one." He grabs the guard's uniform and dresses quickly.

"I'll be sure to give her my best when I see her." I pull the suit on with practiced efficiency. The fit is impeccable, and I almost feel normal again. Almost.

"That should be in about five minutes, except someone decided to chitchat with a guard," Sam grumbles.

"I've cut things closer than this in the past. We'll be fine."

Sam stuffs the custodian coveralls into the bag as I drop my prison suit on top of the unconscious guard.

Now for the unpleasant part. Sam instructs me to tilt my head. My neck flashes with pain as he extracts the tracking chip all inmates have implanted under their skin.

"You still bleed like the rest of us," Sam says and hands me a first-aid patch.

The cool analgesic calms the wound and stems the flow of blood. I straighten my collar to hide it.

Sam tucks the tracking chip into the guard's sock and pulls the incriminating dart from his neck. We then carry his body into the stacks.

"You ready for the walk?" Sam asks. "The paperwork isn't going to match up, so the exit might be tricky."

"We'll be all right," I say. "New man on duty at the gate." This was one reason I chose today for the break.

Together we walk to the library door, which pops open with the badge on Sam's stolen uniform. Beyond lies empty hallway.

"I couldn't cut off the mood system. It's Vigilante," Sam says.

I nod in acknowledgment. We head down the hall, attracting attention with every step. There aren't a lot of sharp suits in prison. Above us, each conduct screen scans us for pulse rate, body temperature, and respiration. We're heading toward the exit with the identification of a person who isn't supposed to even arrive for another three months.

This is where things might get hairy.

4

MIA

Three quick short knocks at the door can only be Shirley, a neighbor from down the road. I shove the prison letter under a book on the desk and rush to the front door.

The dang thing always sticks when the weather turns cool. The autumn air teases the flyaway tendrils around my forehead as Shirley gives a little wave on the porch.

"Brought you a potpie," she says, holding up a

small casserole dish.

I step back so she can pass me to head to the kitchen. Shirley is like everyone else in this small town, weathered, friendly, and nosy to a fault. I follow her through the house, glancing at the hidden letter like its naughty contents might announce themselves.

Shirley slides her dish into the oven and sets the temperature to warm. "You can eat it when you like," she says pleasantly.

Her face is pink cheeked, cherubic, and dimpled. Her gray hair is a mass of curls that she keeps up at Patsy's Beauty Parlor, same as she has since the 1980s. You can see exactly where the little rods line up to produce the waves.

She brushes her hands together. "Starting to feel right like fall out there. You been out today?" Her question is innocent, but I know she's worried that I haven't been going anywhere.

"I stopped by the store for some milk this morning," I say.

She nods and starts moving past me again. "Can't stay for a chat today. Rowdy got fixed this afternoon and he's howling like we've cut off his…"

She pauses. "Well, I guess we did."

She laughs, a merry tinkling sound. Then she whirls around and places a warm hand on each of my cheeks.

"Beatrice thought the world of you. You figure out what it is you want to do next, and I bet the whole town will be right along to help you do it."

I nod against her hands. I have no doubt she's right.

Shirley lets go of my face. "I would feel an awful lot better if you had someone here with you. The Petersons just had a litter of pups. You sure you don't want one? Half husky. Make a good guard dog."

"I'll think about it," I say, although I know having a dog would limit my options. "I might still go back to school."

"Of course," Shirley says. "You're just twenty years old. Lots of life ahead of you."

A long howl breaks the quiet. "Oh, that Rowdy," she says. "You'd think we…" She laughs again. "Hopefully he won't keep you up tonight. We'll keep him inside except when he does his business."

"I'll be fine," I say.

Shirley leans forward and kisses my cheek. "Our poor little Mia," she says. "You know you can always call any of us family."

"Thank you, Shirley," I say. I'm grateful to her. I really am.

She hurries down the steps. A sudden gust of wind stirs up the leaves and they whirl in a tight cone.

Shirley pauses and turns to see if I saw it. "Autumn!" she calls out. "Change is coming!"

She gets in her car and I see Rowdy with his cone of shame. He's managed to get his head out the window even with the wide white brim. He howls again.

Poor dog. It's not far to Shirley's, just across the road and down a piece, but with Rowdy, she didn't walk it. Her old Buick roars to life, and she waves out the open window as she backs down the long drive.

I'm alone again.

I wander the living room, touching each of Aunt Bea's treasured silver bells. I've lived in this sprawling house most of my life, after my parents died when I was eight, so I know every nook and cranny.

I should make some tea. I move to the kitchen and flip on the gas burner for the kettle. The transfer of ownership of the house to me will go through soon, after the execution of the will.

Then I'll have to decide what to do. Sell it, I guess? Rent it? I need to go finish a degree. Do something.

I feel adrift, unmoored, like a boat some sailor accidentally freed by tying a shoddy timber hitch.

The stopper knot thrusts against you,
eliciting another impassioned cry.

Oh, those letters won't let me stop thinking of them.

But they do contain a strange coincidence, which is one reason I kept them.

The knots. I know all the knots.

My parents drilled nautical terms into me as if they were the language of our family. We had a small sailboat that we took out on the lake not far from our home.

As they taught me to handle the boat, I got to know every type of knot, hitch, and heaving line.

Since reading the prison letters, however, some

of the terms have taken on a whole new meaning.

French whipping knot, for example.

Heat flutters through me again. I wish for some sort of history, a bit of sexual experience to draw upon as the emotions flood me while reading the letters. But a tiny public school followed by a small community college hasn't afforded me much opportunity.

Besides, most people find me odd, in a Belle from *Beauty and the Beast* way. Studious, sharp nosed, and more likely to stay up all night reading than attending parties.

Not that I am ever invited.

The kettle whistles. I realize I have neglected to fill the tea ball or place it in a mug. Daydreaming, another bad habit, worsened by my solitude.

I spoon some loose tea into the ball and snap it closed.

The kitchen is forlorn. I open the stove and pull out Shirley's potpie. The lovely aroma of chicken calms me, but I'm not hungry.

I put it away in the fridge and wander through the downstairs, both hands wrapped around a warm mug. The cold is coming, but the chill I feel isn't really about the weather. It's this sense that I am doomed to wander through my life alone. I can't even imagine a life duller than the one I have lived so far.

I pause before an image hanging in the hallway. Me. My parents. I am young, maybe six, happy.

My father wears a sailing hat, his big grin the only thing visible in its shadow.

My mom is beautiful, her hair blowing away from her face, refined and elegant in white shorts and a sweater.

My aunt was my mother's sister. The two of them didn't look anything alike, and from all accounts, didn't act the same either. My mother craved adventure, daring, and met my father when she cut off his catamaran in a local regatta.

My aunt was a kind, slow-paced woman who was never very excitable. Apparently, just like me. When my parents died in a sailing accident, just like everybody said was bound to happen with their lifestyle and their personalities, she took me in.

I head back to the living room, taking small sips of tea. I glance out the windows looking over the lawn.

Another day of my life is passing with nothing

to show for it.

Maybe I should take another look at the letters. Crazy as it sounds, I think my mother would approve.

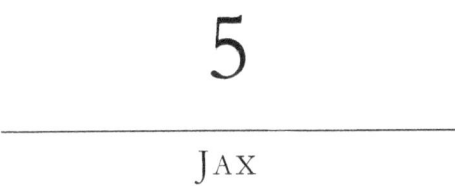

5

JAX

Every head turns as Sam and I saunter through the prison as if we own the place. Inmates sneer at my well-turned suit. Guards peer at Sam as though trying to decide if they know him or not.

The central hub is a maze of glass-walled offices. We stride through, Sam one step ahead of me as escort, and make our way to the check-in desk on the far side. The guard stares at a monitor in front of him. From our angle I can just make out some sort of baseball game. The cord from his earbuds snakes down his chest. He pays us no mind.

Sam clears his throat. "You gonna make us stand here all day?"

After a lingering glance at the screen, the guard finally looks up. He gives us a quick onceover, eyes landing on me. "Who's this?"

"Librarian. Cleaning up our collection," says Sam.

The guard sighs and keys something on his screen. He's got some attitude for only having worked here a few days. A list and schedule replaces the baseball game. "Name?"

"Sergio Avanti," I say.

The guard frowns as he scrolls through the text. I focus on my breathing. Sam huffs and shifts on his feet. Seconds tick by that feel like hours. The guard pauses and stares at his screen. "What the hell?" he asks aloud.

I know he's not seeing any evidence of our check-in. A trained guard would know something is amiss, but we're banking on this new hire not wanting to admit he's confused.

There's also the matter of the Vigilantes. They control the security here. If we stand by this desk too long, if the guard's mood sensor goes off or he keys in something suspicious, they could step in. I've spotted a couple of them mingling with the staff during my year here. If I am caught, protecting Sam and Colette is my utmost imperative.

The mood sensor overhead shifts from green to yellow. Sam and I are fine. It's the guard. I consider how best to calm him down.

"Says here you weren't supposed to come till after Christmas," he says. "Why are you here now?"

"The schedules are always off," Sam says. "Second time this week I've had to escort somebody who doesn't show up onscreen."

The guard stares at the monitor another minute. The mood sensor remains yellow. He glances at my suit as if to convince himself I couldn't possibly be a prisoner. There's no reason to doubt my position, although we did probably overshoot the mark for a prison library volunteer.

His mood sensor starts edging into red. "You look familiar." His voice is tight.

Time to bring this down.

"People often mistake me for the actor Bradford Argetti," I say. Big film star. I look nothing like him.

The guard snorts. "And I look like the King of England."

"I favor Will Smith," Sam says. He pats his good-sized belly, as if the actor ever had an extra pound on him.

This makes the guard laugh. The screen cycles down to yellow, then to green.

He taps a few keys and hits a button to open the steel doors. "Call first next time," he says. "Get the books straight."

"Will do," I say and give him a half salute. "Your Highness."

He laughs again as we pass through to the main lobby.

"Nice save," Sam whispers. "Colette's out front in a black Lexus sedan." As we approach the door, his guard badge goes red. He frowns. "Pick me up at the employee entrance around the corner." He turns and disappears down a side hall.

I resist the urge to glance at the camera bubbles on the ceiling. I pass by the visitor entrance queue and exit through the wide front doors. The sun blinds me momentarily as I squint in search of Colette. I need not wait long. Within seconds, a sleek black sedan pulls up on a silent electric engine. The passenger door pops open.

"Someone call for a lift?" Colette's voice calls from inside, her French accent tickling the words.

I slide into the seat. When the door is closed, I let out a sigh. "You have no idea how good this feels," I say as I sink into the supple leather.

Colette laughs, her dark bob bouncing against her cheeks. "It is good to see you, too, Jax."

"You know how glad I am you're here," I say.

"Sam get stuck?" Concern crosses her brow, a crease forming below the short bangs.

"Employees can't exit the front," I say. "I warned him."

"He thought he rerouted that badge."

"Go around the corner," I say. "He'll be along." I have utter faith in Sam's ability to get out of a tight spot. Besides, he's a legitimate Vigilante. Unless they tie him to me immediately, he's golden.

Colette inches the car along the front of the compound, then pulls around to the side. We both scan the gates for openings, side exits, and vulnerable spots in case we have to make a hard getaway.

Minutes tick by.

"Where is he?" Her voice has an edge of fear.

"We had to kill communication since we could be overheard."

The door opens, but instead of Sam, Johnson comes out. He spots the black car and heads straight for us.

"Are we compromised?" Colette asks. "Should we go?" She reaches for the acceleration switch.

I hold out my arm to stop her. "I am not leaving Sam."

Johnson comes right up to the blacked-out window to peer in. As soon as his nose is close to the glass, I open the door with enough force to break his nasal bone.

He falls back in a stagger, blood dripping down his face. I step out of the car and wait for him to look up.

"Shit," he says. "You?"

"The one and only," I say. I'm not interested in getting his blood on my new suit, so instead of hitting him again, I pinch the nerve in his neck that will drop him cleanly.

His knees buckle. I don't bother to spare him from collapsing facedown on the asphalt.

Sam smashes through the door. "Get ready to roll," he calls out. Behind him are two other guards.

I step back inside the car. "Impeccable timing," I tell him.

"Go," he says as he dives into the backseat.

Colette wheels us away. The guards give chase for a moment, but once Colette punches the nitrous acceleration, they fall behind. One stops to speak into his lapel radio. Won't matter. In moments we are past the gate.

"Nice work, you two," I say. "I owe you both a drink."

"Cut it too close," says Sam from the backseat, "so you can add that to our tab. Hope your money's good." He rolls down the window and tosses his guard badge out onto the asphalt.

"Always," I say. Not that Sam needs money. Every Vigilante has access to any amount necessary, without question.

Sam claps my shoulder. "God damn, it's good to have you back," he says.

"It's been too quiet without you around," adds Colette. She downshifts the car back into normal drive mode. "What's your plan now?"

I watch the scenery whip by out the window for a second. "I need to get to Klaus. I think Jovana's on to him."

"Still the thing with that woman?" Colette's voice holds a laugh.

I frown. "I killed an innocent man because of her."

"Not so innocent," Colette says.

"Neither of them," I say. My stomach burns just thinking of Jovana. I loved that woman. Stupidly. Foolishly. To my doom. She used me to kill one of her rivals, a fellow Vigilante. That act landed me in prison. Only Sam, Colette, and Klaus know the truth. Jovana vanished after getting my hands dirty.

"I think she has Klaus," I say.

"He was lying low, no?" says Colette. "How do you know he's been compromised?" I sense the worry in her voice.

"His letters. They weren't right," I say.

"You and your bondage," Colette says, shaking her head. "Klaus probably got his knickers in a knot just trying to keep it all straight."

I glance back at Sam, who stares out the window, his dark face clouded with concern. "Klaus is a smart man," he says. "He can manage a little code."

"I agree," I say. "We need to get to the

Tennessee safe house."

"We can't go with you," says Sam. "We've taken enough risk with the syndicate for one day."

He's right. They jeopardized their positions as Vigilantes for me.

"Then drop me off. I need to check on him."

"Already planned for," Colette says. She glances in the rearview mirror at Sam. "Get out of that suit, Sam. It's probably got some sort of sensor."

"Nah. It's civilian," Sam says, but still he strips off the guard uniform. As we pass over a river, he rolls down the window and lets it fly.

"Sam! Litterbug!" Colette is indignant.

"Toss the suit! Don't litter!" Sam tries to sound mad, but the Louisiana lilt to his voice belies the humor.

I sit back in the seat, savoring the sights. One year in that hellhole. The only view was the straight-up look at the sky while out on the grounds. Now Chicago stretches out in all directions. Pubs. Restaurants. Long rows of houses fitted close together. The El.

"I'm taking you as far as the suburbs," Colette says. "There we meet up with our clone IDs."

35

"I was wondering how you went off grid," I say.

Sam pulls a knit shirt down over his chest. "You've been in the clink, boss. Been a lot of tech upgrades in the syndicate while you were out of commission." He taps a leather suitcase beside him on the backseat. "Inside here are all the tools we predicted you might need while you avoid the network. There's an audio rundown on them for you to listen to on the drive."

I nod appreciatively. Sam is the gadget man, even if he can be old school about it. He often chooses a hammer over a retina scan, but he always knows the latest Vigilante tech. His ability to circumvent it with no more than a loose wire and a pair of pliers has saved us more times than I can count.

Colette has always been our getaway girl. She can maneuver anything with wheels, wings, sails, or engine.

"This Lexus is stolen, and the identifier chip is attached to a jelly brick in the trunk to give it some mass," Colette says. "I'd say you've got three days on this ID before he surfaces."

I don't ask about the status of the man whose

identity I'll be borrowing. When Colette says "surfaces," it could mean anything, and it's probably better I don't know.

Sam points at the front dash. "I've set up a countdown on the ID." A red display projects seventy hours onto the windshield.

"I think you should give up on the woman," Colette says, a bitter edge to her voice.

I try to sound cool and impassive, not that it fools her. "The syndicate is going to come after me," I say. "Jovana's the only shot I have at clearing my name."

I have zero future if the Vigilantes don't back me on this, and they all know it.

Sam leans forward. "Jovana's been off grid the whole year. Nobody can track her, not even the syndicate."

"That's impossible," I say.

"She's obviously got friends in high-tech places," Sam says.

Colette reaches over to squeeze my arm. "We'll help as we can," she says. "All the letters are scanned and in the system."

"Thanks," I say. Colette does always remember every last detail.

"We're approaching our rendezvous with our clones." Colette touches a yellow button on the screen in the dash. "You can play the letters back here. Perhaps get more ideas."

I doubt I will learn much more than I did in prison, with nothing else to do but study the strange rearrangement of my code in handwriting that does not match any of the styles Klaus adopted.

"I know what a risk you two took to get me out," I say to Colette. "I won't forget it."

"We won't let you forget it," Sam says with a laugh.

Colette exits the freeway and approaches a small gas station. This Lexus is electric, but as we approach, a hybrid Mustang wheels out from behind the pumps.

"That's our ride," Sam says. "You're letting me drive this one."

Colette rolls her eyes. "I'll try not to get bored." She leans over and kisses my cheek. "Be safe, Jax. We'll catch up with you again in three days."

"Be careful out there," Sam says. "There's a blackout phone in the bag. It's a rare bird. Don't use it unless you have to."

I nod. Colette and Sam walk away toward the Mustang. Two other people get out of the car and head into the station.

I open the passenger door slowly, breathing in the smell of gasoline and autumn. Leaves skitter across the broken pavement.

I walk around to the front of the car, fingers lightly grazing the smooth glossy surface of the hood. It is an excellent vehicle and well equipped. I am out of prison, and on my way to clearing up this little matter that made the Vigilantes overreact so abominably. Time to head to the Tennessee safe house and see who is impersonating Klaus, or holding him as some sort of hostage.

Whoever it is, they'd better be ready for me.

6

MIA

Another long empty night has arrived. I feel disjointed and unsettled. Maybe it's the letters. Maybe it's the change of seasons.

I wonder how Aunt Bea ended up here all her life, never married, alone in this rambling old house.

I have to be careful or it could happen to me.

I check both doors. Locked tight. Not that it matters. This small town has all the danger of a potted plant.

But for some reason Aunt Bea has enough deadbolts for Fort Knox. I run my fingers over the cold steel. It takes six different keys to open them all. Maybe the first thing to do now that she's gone is to have all but one of them removed. I will be fearless, like my mother. I won't stay locked away.

I head back to my small bedroom. There's nothing to stop me from taking over my aunt's larger one, but it doesn't feel quite right. Not yet.

I flip on the light. My room is tidy with its smooth crocheted bedspread, small dresser, and wicker nightstand. A bit of high school memorabilia still hangs on a bulletin board. I was president of the chess club.

Yes, the dullest life ever.

Except...the letters. I have placed the older ones in a wooden box on my nightstand. I run my finger over the carvings on the lid of the box, wondering if I should read through them again. So unusual, talking about all that bondage and using nautical terms. So intriguing and sexy and strange.

I lay back on the bed, imagining in my mind the person who writes them. Jax De Luca.

Does he hunch over a metal desk scattered with paper and pens? I wonder if he has a book of knots that he refers to as he writes, or if, like me, he has knowledge of them from years of study.

The letters are always addressed to "Klaus" on the envelope. Inside, each begins with a broad-stroked "K." Whoever K. Klaus is, this Jax guy is really into her. Kate? Kathryn? Karen?

When I found the first one in my aunt's unsorted mail, I set it aside, planning to return it. But weeks passed, and one day in a flurry of going through letters to find a missing bill, I accidentally opened the envelope.

By the time I read the first line, I was hooked. I searched through a newer stack, and sure enough, a second one was buried in the pile.

I read them, again and again. The knots made them so personal, like they were meant for me.

And they were so sexy. I'd never read anything like it. It's as though they unlocked some secret part of me. Forbidden. Hot. Exciting.

On one of my quiet days, I drove out to the local library, and hidden behind a fern, opened up that popular bondage book *Fifty Shades of Grey* to see if maybe the letter writer was just copying passages from it. I had gleaned from bits of news that filtered in from neighbors that this scandalous novel had the same sort of subject matter.

But no, the words were all his own.

I would never have written him back, except I kept passing that picture in the hallway. Mother, so beautiful and brave, fearless and full of adventure. How much harm could come from a letter? And wasn't it a kindness? I would be easing the plight of some poor incarcerated soul.

Obviously his K. Klaus lied to him about her whereabouts, as this address has been owned by my aunt for decades. She probably distanced herself after his trial.

I tried looking up the prisoner's name. I found very little. No arrest. No crime. Just a small notice about his arrival at Ridley Prison. No picture. Just his age, 37, and birth city, Atlanta. Also a Southerner. He would serve fifteen years of a sixty-year sentence. Only a year had passed.

Surely if he did something truly terrible, there would be news about it. Probably he was some white-collar criminal who evaded taxes or laundered funds, and the company kept it quiet to avoid upsetting the shareholders.

Or so I told myself.

My first attempts to write him fell flat. I

couldn't quite bring the sexy into the knots. So I began to copy his letters word for word, then slowly rearrange the sentences and switch out the knots. But the time I managed a draft I was pleased with, my urge to share it was strong.

So I mailed it.

Shirley's dog howls in the night, a long terrible wail. I sit straight up in my bed. Rowdy never makes any noise, not that I can hear down the road. The howl is followed by a series of barks, then he goes quiet. He must have tried to relieve himself in the yard, and it wasn't pleasant for him after his snipping. Poor dog.

I relax back against the headboard.

I turn to the box of letters, wondering if I can handle reading one more before I go to sleep. Maybe my dreams will be full of Jax De Luca and his slipknots.

I lift my hand in the air, the long cotton sleeve of the old-fashioned nightgown sliding to my elbow. I giggle, imagining my wrist tethered to the bedpost. I shift my ankles apart beneath the comforter. They don't quite make the width of the bed to reach the knobs on the corners. The long skirt of the gown keeps me from spreading very wide.

I'm just not the sort of girl made for BDSM novels.

But Jax doesn't know that.

I pick up a pencil and jot down one new idea that has just come to me with my movements on the bed.

You jerk my ankles apart with such strength that my gown disintegrates into tattered shreds around my naked hips.

I shudder at the thought of it. Now it will be hard to go to sleep. I set the pencil and paper back on the nightstand and flip off the light. In the dark, the night is quiet, a silence I am used to. Tomorrow I will try to sort through my life, figure out my next step. Somewhere out there is a future for me. I just never thought to plan for it.

My eyes are heavy. For a little while, I drift in a twilight sleep. The letters ruffle through my thoughts. The cool silk of a well-made rope sliding around my wrist. The tickle of a sheet as it slips across my body.

Then I'm awake.

Wide awake.

The light on me is harsh.

My arms are immobile.

Both wrists are tight against the bedposts.

My breasts and belly are crisscrossed with red rope over my white gown.

One ankle is tethered to the knob at the base of the bed.

My other leg is in the air, lifted by an arm.

An arm in a slick pale gray suit.

A suit connected to a man with a scruffy beard and dark, impenetrable eyes.

"Good evening," says a deep voice.

Oh, God. Who is it?

I can't speak. I can't breathe.

My nightgown is riding up, exposing my leg. The man tucks my ankle on his shoulder.

I begin to hyperventilate, my chest heaving. This isn't happening. Not in my town. Not to me. It's a dream. A bad dream.

I try to look at the man, to see inside those hooded eyes.

He waits, patiently, for me to come fully awake.

It's not a dream. Men in fancy suits don't wait for you to wake up in dreams.

"Who…are…you?" I finally ask.

"I think you know who I am." He reaches down for the sheaf of letters and flings them across my body.

"Jax?"

"The one and only."

"But you're in prison." My eyes dart to my body, the rope, the white pages, and his lean body in the silk suit.

His grin spreads wide.

"Not anymore."

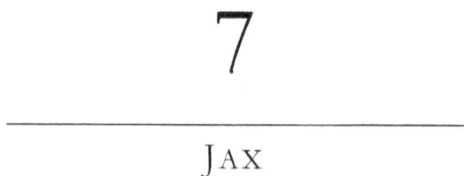

7

J AX

I hold fast to the woman's ankle. What sort of spy is this? Vigilante? Counterintelligence? She isn't trained like any operative I've ever seen.

Except one.

Jovana.

My anger burns hot at the thought of it.

Her honey-brown hair splays across a white pillow. Her terror is palpable. So real. Does she have some sort of mood enhancement capability?

Her fright prickles my protective urges, and I have to stuff it down to maintain control.

Damn this vexation. I was at the highest pinnacle of the syndicate before Jovana. I'm not aware of this level of training. Now I'm out of the loop. Susceptible.

Her breaths are rapid and short. She seems on the verge of hyperventilating.

So convincing. Damn it.

"Tell me who you work for," I bark at her.

Her eyes squeeze shut. "I don't work," she says, her voice raspy. "I was just watching out for my aunt."

"Who is your aunt?"

Her throat moves as she tries to swallow. She's good. I pin her ankle against my shoulder. This damn old-fashioned nightgown is in my way.

I flick my wrist, activating a hidden holster in my sleeve. A slender dagger falls into my hand. I slice the long skirt of her gown to the knee.

She gives a little yelp. Her face is pink, and her wide green eyes fasten on me. "My aunt is Beatrice Carina," she says quickly. "She died two weeks ago."

"Who killed her?" I ask, none too kindly.

"N-no one," the woman says. "She had another stroke."

"I assume you won't identify yourself." I grip her ankle in a vise that I know will bruise. To her credit, she doesn't even wince. This element of her training is solid.

"I'm Mia," she says. "Mia Morrow."

I drop her leg to the bed and tug out the updated Identipad Sam packed in the case. It has been listening to the entire conversation and making cross-references. Paragraphs line up on the screen. I keep an eye on the woman as I scan it. She may be skilled in escaping silk-rope bondage.

Though it does look good on her. Something about the crimson rope on the lacy cotton gown makes my blood rush. The year of enforced celibacy weighs on me. Despite the information flashing across my Identipad, my eyes casually slide up her ankle, the slim calf, the smooth knee, and the beginnings of a soft thigh. She makes me want to cut more of the gown.

But for now, I must assess her skills. She isn't muscular or taut. So, not trained for military combat or fighting. Her talents must lie in her manipulation. Cunning. Mood-enhanced speech.

I am already distracted by her skin. Damn it to hell. They've sent another Jovana, another damsel in distress. False innocence. They think I will be that stupid again.

Rage blasts through me.

"You're a liar," I growl at the girl. The Identipad lists the owner of the safe house as Georgiana Powers, part of the Mason-Dixon syndicate. She vacated the house only six months ago.

The woman tries to sit up against the bonds, but fails, falling back. More thigh shows. I'm definitely distracted. They must have sent this one particularly for me. She matches my every preference in women. Honey hair. Petite. Skilled.

"Look it up in the paper," she cries. "Her funeral was at the Baptist church. She was my only family."

I ignore her prepared story, unmoved by its expert presentation. Mia Morrow comes up next, and this woman's image. So she isn't lying about that. But there is no history of her. It's a blank slate. She's wiped. No identification beyond her name and gender.

Just like Jovana.

I'm livid.

"You will talk to me," I say, and slice the dagger through the white gown again. Now it's slit high on her thigh. "Who are you, really?"

"Mia!" she cries. She pushes back against her pillow, as if she can escape me.

"Who wrote the letters?"

At that, she sags limply, her expression dropping into shame. "I did. I shouldn't have. I—I led you on. I pretended to be K. Klaus."

This makes me laugh out loud, ringing through the room with such force that the girl lurches away, banging against the headboard.

"Do you even know who Klaus is?" I ask.

She squirms against the wrist binding. "I assumed it was the woman you are in love with."

I tuck the dagger back into my wrist holster and lift a polished shoe up on the base of the bed. I lean over, bracing my arm on one knee. I don't know who this Mia girl is, but she poses no threat to me.

"Klaus is my partner. He came to this safe house to wait on my instructions. The letters were for him."

"You—you like men?" she asks, still not

understanding anything.

I drop my foot and come around to the side of the bed. She wiggles a little so that she can cross her loose leg over the slit in her gown, as if she is trying to preserve her modesty.

Whatever. I know how girls like her are trained. The innocent victim. They want to ensnare you, like a pool shark pretends to be a beginner.

But this one wrote me in my own code, which means she knew what she was doing, however pathetically she misinterpreted the knots.

I will show her I understand her game, and that I am not a Vigilante to be trifled with. We'll end this little charade here and now.

I sit next to her. Her breathing speeds up again. The letters are still spread across the bed. I spot one with only a single line. "A new one?" I ask. "For me?"

She doesn't answer, just watches with those green eyes. Vixen eyes. Looks like I'll be ending my dry spell on this one before it's over. Maybe I'll let her think she's seducing me, right till the end.

I pick up the letter.

"Let's see," I say. "What was on sweet Mia's mind before she retired this evening?" I hold the paper to the light. "Mmmm. I like this. 'You jerk my ankles apart with such strength that my gown disintegrates into tattered shreds around my naked hips.'"

I glance down at her thighs. "I say we give this one a go."

Her eyes widen with shock. Such a well-trained little actress. I look forward to assessing her skill. What sort of maneuvers does she take pride in? I can already picture those slender legs wrapped around me.

I grasp the white cotton and tear it past her waist. Her hips are narrow in simple white panties. I finger the lace edge. Her breathing comes fast again. She's so good at this. I almost believe it.

"Such pretty little underwear," I say.

Her green eyes glisten with tears. So well done.

"Are you going to tell me you're a virgin?" I ask. "I hope you know you can only do the hymen restructure surgery so many times before you lose feeling."

Her mouth opens in a feigned oval of shock. As if she didn't know.

"Your nightclothes remind me of one of my favorite books. *Little Women*. Have you read it?"

She shakes her head no.

"A pity," I say. "Such strong women in that book. Do you consider yourself a strong woman?"

She shakes her head again.

"Too bad. Because we're about to find out what you're made of."

When I rip another slice through her nightgown, she screams.

8

MIA

I am in hell.

I am in the hell I deserve for lying to this man.

For writing him.

For leading him on.

I wish I had never seen the letters. Never thought about them.

Never written back.

I can't watch him cut up my gown. It's too frightening, so I squeeze my eyes shut. I know he's looking at me. The air is hitting my thighs and belly. I'm typically shy. No one has ever seen this much of me.

His slipknots on my wrists are perfectly tied, so that the more I move, the tighter they get.

I don't recognize the pattern across my body, however.

These aren't sailing knots. They are something else, meant for other purposes.

I don't have to see them to remember how they look. The blood-red ropes crisscrossing my breasts and ribs aren't something I'll easily forget. The image is branded on my brain.

I won't open my eyes. I don't want to see my shredded nightgown. He used my own words against me, slicing the gown apart like we were lovers on a dare.

Goosebumps spread across my skin from the chill. I'm embarrassed as much as scared. The bed shifts as he moves.

I assume he will take me now, do what he wants to me. He'll assume my real virginity is — what did he call it?

Hymen restructuring?

Where does this man come from?

I don't know if he will kill me. He seems so well dressed for a murderer, so gentlemanly in how he talks, even when he's accusing me of lying.

Jax De Luca. Who is he? How did he get out of jail?

He assumed my aunt had been murdered. This must be his life.

Moments pass, and still, nothing. My thighs grow weary of clenching together. Is he not going to do anything?

Now I'm not sure what I feel. Disappointment? Surely not. But something eases. The terror drops a notch.

Carefully, slowly, I open one eye.

Jax is watching me with amusement. "That's all you've got?" he says. "Clenching in fear? Surely you've finished at least Phase One training if you're in a safe house."

I don't know what he means.

My thigh muscle cramps, and I'm forced to let my loose leg down. The other one is still tied to the bedpost.

"I mean, that was a very convincing scream," he goes on. "But I had expected something more…titillating."

Anger blossoms in me. What the hell does he want from me? Some grand seduction?

"I'm not exactly in a position to manhandle you." I wiggle my fingers in the bonds.

He laughs again, less forcefully this time. It's actually sort of…charming.

"So you write about bondage but you can't escape it?"

I finally get the courage to glance down at my body. My thighs peek through a tangle of white strips. My panties are in full view.

The nightgown is more fitting of a prostitute now. My face flames with embarrassment. I cross one leg over the other again. I don't care how much they cramp.

"You were right about the gown," Jax says. "Can't spread very wide in that awkward thing." The one-line letter lies between us like an accusation. "I fixed it for you."

His gaze travels the length of my body, pausing on my breasts, which are fat and round inside the crisscross of the rope binding. Thankfully the white gown is thick and hides how my nipples pucker up as he looks at me. A rush of heat blasts through my body. Despite what is happening, I feel a tingle, like parts of me are waking up for the first time.

Something beeps in the corner of the room. We both turn.

Jax walks over to the lampshade on my dresser and pulls a small oval-shaped device from inside.

"What is that?" I ask.

He stares at it. "Well, this safe house is compromised," he says darkly. "Good thing I already pilfered the stockpile."

"What are you talking about?"

"You deny it to the end." He shakes his head as he reaches for the slipknot at my wrist and expertly unwinds it from the bedpost. My arm drops to the bed. I can't even move it, so little blood is flowing.

"Are you letting me go?" I ask as he reaches across me for the other arm. He smells expensive, like fine clothes and luxury cars. I stifle the urge to inhale deeply.

"Oh, no. You're coming with me." He unties my ankle.

As soon as my leg is free, I snap my knees together. He tilts his head. "A little late for modesty," he says.

I kick at the sheets and pile them around me,

creating a shield.

Jax laughs. "If I know your type, we're going to be carnally acquainted very soon." He leans over and holds my chin tight in his grip. "I am happy to take advantage of whatever skills you want to test on me, but don't think your wiles are going to get you anywhere."

His face moves in super close, just inches from mine. I can't breathe, his lips are so near. If I leaned forward, I could kiss him, feel the stubble of his cheek. I want to. I don't care what he's done, breaking into my house, tying me up. I want that kiss.

I'm losing my mind. He's a stranger. A convicted felon. I can't want this. I can't want him.

He pulls away and jerks at the ties still encircling my wrists. He tugs my hands behind my back, locking them down with the binding on my waist. The rope makes a sizzling sound as he pulls it through, and I shiver. I should not be feeling so attracted to this man. I try to summon my fear and anger, but I'm still on fire from his closeness, and how what he's doing matches his letters.

"Can you stand?" he asks.

I scoot to the edge of the bed and manage to

get on my feet. The tattered gown falls around my legs.

"Almost perfect," Jax says. He reaches for the collar of my gown. "But let's not forget exactly who and what you are." He rips the lace neckline, pulling it wide until the cleavage created by the ropes threatens to spill out.

"That's more like the vixen I expect," he says.

I can't be insulted. He's right. I wrote him those sexy things. I told him this is what I wanted. He's only doing what I asked him to. I had begged to be tied up, treated like a whore. And taken roughly, passionately, until I screamed.

Good God. Was that next?

For a moment his fingers slide along my collarbone, then down to the hollow between my breasts. I can barely breathe, suspended between terror and wild attraction. He could have done anything to me, yet he hasn't. I don't know what to think of him. Gentleman or rogue? Killer or hero?

The beeps from his device come faster.

"Time to fly," he says. He slides the end of the rope through the binding in front and leads me out of my bedroom like I'm a slave. I don't even have a chance to look back. Whatever future I imagined when I went to bed last night is long gone.

For now, at least, it seems I belong to Jax.

9

JAX

I drag this Mia person through the house. I've already been through most of it. Aside from the emergency stockpile that looks fairly untouched, hidden beneath the floor of the kitchen pantry, the house contains nothing tying it to the Vigilantes.

The detector in her bedroom is old, decades old. Still, it tells me the safe house is being monitored. This woman has to know it was there.

Unfortunately, the house holds no clues

regarding the possible whereabouts of Klaus. Where could he have gone? Did he skip out with Jovana on his heels? Did she catch him and leave this tartlet behind to trap me? My anger flares again at the thought. Jovana must think me stupid to fall for such a ploy. Again.

I jerk the rope and Mia protests with a startled "Hey!"

"Dragging you is just as easy. Less comfortable for you, though. I suggest you keep up."

She glares at me, the innocent vixen act gone. This girl has some toughness in her. I'm going to enjoy learning every facet of her training and personality. But I *will* get the facts from her, one way or another.

We cross the living room and I realize that Klaus must still be free, but Jovana obviously knew he was here at one point. She must have left Mia behind to keep watch.

The records say Powers left six months ago. Shortly before my first letter to Klaus. I puzzle the timeline together in my head. Powers leaves, my letter arrives, Mia intercepts it and responds as Klaus. A trap to extract information from me, either through the letters or in person.

Clever, Jovana. But you're slipping. Your lackey temptress needs work.

I pause by the back door and peer out the small window. No movement.

I look back at Mia. Her wide green eyes stare back. I wrap the rope around my fist and pop my knife from its wrist sheath. To her credit, she doesn't flinch as I slice off one of the tattered scraps from her nightgown.

"Turn around," I order. She complies and I catch a glimpse of her thighs as the strips of cloth sway with her movement.

Focus, Jax.

"Hold still." I knot the center of the strip and gag her with it, tying the cloth around her head. It's tight enough that she can't work it free, but loose enough not to cut into her cheeks. She may be wearing it a while. I can't have her alerting her allies to our departure.

"We're going to take a little walk now. We can't slow down. I was not kidding about dragging you if I need to. Nod if you understand."

Mia nods and a tremble passes through her. Well played. I almost feel sorry for her.

Almost.

Back at the door, I strap on a night-vision monocle. Too bad I don't have a tracer. The car is across the field, a long way to walk in the open. Plenty of opportunity for anyone to spot us.

No time to worry about that now.

Mia mumbles something and gestures with her bare foot at a pair of Crocs by the door. My first thought is to make her walk barefoot, but the rocks and sticks in the field may cut her feet. That would both slow us down and leave a trail of DNA blood evidence.

I nod, and she slips the shoes on. Then we're out on the porch.

We double-time it across the dark yard and into a field. I force us to stay low as I scan the area with my night-vision eye. Nothing moves but I do not trust my limited senses.

The warning beeps from the security device in the house could have meant anything. Someone close. Someone there. Or someone just watching. It was an old model. Klaus should have updated it. Unless he couldn't.

I pull Mia along as fast as I dare. The unstable dirt shifts beneath my feet and forces me to slow more than I would like.

Mia stumbles several times and falls to her knees once, but I pull her back up and move her along. Her breath comes in rasps through the gag by the time we reach the tree line on the far side of the field. The car sits a short distance down a dirt road, and a quick tap on my watch unlocks the doors. I push her into the rear seat and secure her with the extra length of rope through metal hooks along the seat back.

Only once we are both inside the car do I reach around and pull off the gag. Mia coughs and works her jaw.

"You didn't have to gag me," she says with a trace of indignation. "I would have been quiet."

"Of course you would," I say.

I maneuver the car down the dirt road, relying on the night vision to guide me. When we turn onto the paved road, I increase in speed and drive without headlights for several miles.

The way is quiet and we pass no cars. Satisfied we are safely away, I toss the monocle onto the passenger seat, hit the lights, and drive more reasonably.

"So where are we going?" Mia asks. Her voice

is less timid now. She must be dropping the victim act.

It's a good question, but I ignore it. I am beginning to doubt Klaus saw any of my letters, or only the first one at best. Everything I gleaned from the responses was wrong. This girl didn't understand the code and bungled the job. I can't shake the nagging feeling that Klaus is in serious trouble.

Sam and Colette got no word from him. He has become a ghost, off the grid and hiding. My meager resources at hand may do me no good in tracking him down. I need more power at my fingertips.

And for that I will need the Vigilantes. A trip into the lion's den. Where is the closest silo?

I tap my watch and bark a command. A faint translucent map of the area appears on the windshield display.

"Identify closest silo to current position." The map zooms out and a circle appears fifty miles away, spinning lazily. Too close. I need more distance between myself and the compromised safe house.

"Next result."

The map zooms out farther, a second circle

appearing to the west in Missouri. Perfect.

"We're going to St. Louis," I tell Mia.

"What's in St. Louis? Klaus?"

I let a chuckle slip out. "Only if I'm lucky."

"What's a silo?"

"A place to store grain." Two can play dumb. "You're a country girl, you know that."

"But that's not the kind of silo you're looking for, is it?" she says. "Because I could show you one, if that's what you want."

"I want the truth, Mia. Who are you working for? Where is Klaus?"

Her voice rises a notch in anger. "I don't work for anyone. You're too numb skulled to realize I have nothing to do with this."

I glance at her in the rearview mirror. Her hair is scattered across the seat. Her chest is heaving, provocative in the slashed white gown and red rope.

"Who taught you knots?" I ask.

She hesitates, then says, "My parents."

"Names?" She gives me two. I put the car on assisted drive and pull out the Identipad. Both her parents come up. Deceased, but like Mia they have no records. Three members of a family, all wiped.

There is a lot more to this girl than meets the

eye. The Vigilantes are protecting her identity from one of their own.

I turn around in the seat and stare at her. She shrinks into the leather under my gaze. My eyes shift to her legs, now tightly pressed together. Her pale skin glows in the dim light, the scraps of her nightgown doing little to hide her.

She sees my gaze and adjusts her body to rearrange the strips in a futile attempt at modesty. So now we're back to innocence. I don't get her. Her actions don't match up with any training protocol I know.

"Who are you, Mia Morrow?" I ask, irritated. "Who are you, really? You have no records. Your parents have no records. Your so-called aunt has no records. The only people who are as blank as you are a special brand of Vigilantes. But you are too young for that treatment."

"I don't understand. Records? Vigilantes?"

My anger flares again. This little game is getting old.

"Cut the act," I snap. "I'm not falling for it. You have some natural skill, I will give you that, but your training failed to prepare you for the real thing. Life will be easier for you if you just tell me what I need to know."

This gets her.

"I don't know what you want!" she cries. She tries to sit up as straight as the rope binding allows. "I'm Mia, just Mia!" Her words come in little stumbling bursts.

We pass a lonely farmhouse and she watches it pass. This seems to break her, as now her voice is full of tears. "I'm not some spy! I don't know who Klaus is or where he is. I don't know who you are, or what you're doing, or that I was writing coded letters, or…"

Her voice fades out. The torn nightgown slips off one shoulder and comes dangerously close to uncovering her breast. I let my gaze linger on her smooth, slight collarbone for a moment. I feel a wave of desire pulse through me.

Manipulated. Not real. Don't fall for it.

I turn my attention back to the road and take over driving. We ride in silence as the minutes and the miles tick by. I hear her take in a deep breath, like she's steadying herself.

"You said Klaus was your partner," she finally says, her voice soft and subdued.

"Yes."

"When did you last see him?"

Another snide remark rests on my tongue but I bite it back. "Over a year ago. The night we were betrayed."

"What happened to you?"

"I went to prison."

"No, I mean what happened when you were betrayed?"

"That's not relevant right now."

"How do you know Klaus is alive, then?"

"He left a message for me in the house," I lie. I don't know that he is alive, not really. But Mia's letters and her presence tell me he is.

"How? My aunt lived there for years! Did he know my aunt?"

"You tell me."

"I..." Mia gives a little grunt of frustration. "Well, what does the note say? Didn't he give you some clue where to go?"

"No, he..."

I stop myself. Stupid, Jax. She almost caught you in your lie. Alarm shoots through me like ice water in my veins. Why is she asking these questions? Nothing I say could help her right now. Unless it's for someone else's benefit.

Of course. It all makes sense. The ease of capturing her and our escape. Her helpless ploy. Her questions and dodges. She wants me to talk so someone else can hear.

I slam on the brakes and pull to the side of the road. Mia gives a yelp as the car jerks and bounces through rows of a grain field. I pull to a stop behind a large tractor.

I jump out and yank her door open. Fury at myself and Jovana burns in my chest as I jerk the rope from the seat ties.

"Get out," I say, my voice cold and harsh.

Mia scrambles out the door as best she can, the ropes limiting her movement. I grab the back of the bindings and pull her tight against me. Her skin is hot against my fingers.

"You're wired," I hiss in her ear.

"What?" she cries. "What are you—"

I turn my fist and the ropes tighten. The silk cords press into her soft skin and Mia gasps.

"I suggest you be very quiet, unless you want the gag again. Nod if you understand."

Mia nods several times in quick succession. I release my grip and turn her around. I flick my wrist to snap the dagger from its sheath into my hand. I hold it between us.

"Now," I say. "You've got a transmitter on you somewhere, and I'm going to find it. I recommend standing very, very still."

10

MIA

I do what he says and stand completely still. The night is chilly, though, and I'm not wearing much. I try to suppress my shivers.

Little ripping sounds signal the cotton getting sliced through. Fresh air hits more skin.

He's cutting my gown away.

We're in the middle of nowhere. He's gone off the highway. There's nothing for miles except empty fields, the occasional parked plow just a shadow in the moonlight.

He could rape me. Kill me. Do anything.

But I'm oddly calm. I think of my mother, her strong smile. Nothing got to her.

What would she do?

Laugh at him. She would show no fear.

He tugs at the strips of my nightgown, pulling them through the ropes that still crisscross my body. He works swiftly, carefully, and the cotton slides across my skin like a caress.

I look down, fascinated, as he tugs it away, revealing my body in the bluish light. White fabric litters the ground at my feet.

He examines each piece, frowning. His face is drawn tight in concentration as he squeezes every white strip. He looks at each button as he pops it from what once was the front of the gown.

The last section covering my chest pulls away with his sharp tug. I might as well be a mannequin for all Jax notices as my breasts are revealed in the moonlight. I stare at myself, my bare body in the red ropes. I shiver with something more than the cold. I'm not sure I've ever felt more alive than I do at this moment. The tears and the fright just drop away, like the pieces of my silly frumpy nightgown.

My mother feels very close. I shove anything away that doesn't help me. No fear. No crying.

Determination. Guile. Be like the letters. Be the girl who wrote them. I have it in me. It was the birthright I gave up when my parents died. I could have been like my mother and father, wild and dangerous. But I chose to live like my aunt.

No more.

Jax twists the last pieces of fabric in his hands. He walks quickly to the trunk of his car, opens it, and pulls some small device from a suitcase. He returns and passes a slender silver wand over the pile of fabric. Nothing happens.

He looks up at me. I've never been more vulnerable in my life. Naked other than the ropes and my panties, freezing in the wind. But I feel strong.

He notices me this time, like he senses something has changed. His eyes linger on my body. I don't feel cold at all now, flush with his gaze. Heat blossoms through my body, growing painfully fiery between my legs. His eyes are shadowed, but he takes his time.

Even in the low light I can see something twitch in his jaw. I don't know what it means, but it's making me feel crazy. I want him to touch me, to do something. It's the most insane sensation I can imagine.

But he didn't hurt me or do anything before, when he could have. He seems to think I'm his enemy, and yet, he's done nothing to harm me.

I no longer fear him.

He steps in closer and I suck in a breath. My heart is hammering so hard he can surely hear it. But he doesn't reach out with his hand. The wand skims the surface of my skin, so close it almost touches.

I'm so sensitized that I almost cry out when he grazes my shoulder. My breathing is fast again. When he says, "Feet wide," I almost can't comprehend his command.

But I take a step out and the device makes its close path up my leg. I almost long for it to touch me, for him to be unable to resist. But he's careful, and doesn't make any contact with the panties or my thighs.

He steps back, arms crossed over the gray suit, watching me.

The cold grips me. I feel brazen enough to say, "You could have just used your wand while I was still wearing the gown."

His laugh ripples across the empty fields. "This was much more enjoyable." He shakes his head. "I don't think I've captured a Phase One Trainee quite as beautiful as you before."

He thinks I'm beautiful. He's the first person to ever say it.

The wind picks up, tossing my hair around. With my hands bound, I can't move it off my face. I try to picture myself in the red ropes, standing in the moonlit field with this dangerous, ungodly handsome man.

Something odd is happening to me. I'm almost naked, wrapped in red rope, hands tied, completely vulnerable.

And yet I feel more powerful than I have ever felt in my entire life. I'm not Mia anymore, not the one curling up alone in her old-fashioned nightgown. I'm a woman who gets into dangerous liaisons with strange men who strip her down to bondage rope and doesn't flinch.

"So, Mr. Jax De Luca," I say in a voice I'm not quite sure is my own. "You've got me right where you want me. But you have no information, no clue about your missing Klaus, and you've kidnapped and stripped an innocent woman in a field. What are you going to do now?"

Jax continues to watch me. His eyes are dark and unreadable in the moonlight.

"I like you, Mia." His eyes drift along my body. "I like you a lot."

I feel like I'm on fire. I have nothing to lose here. If he was going to hurt me, he already would have. I take a timid step forward and lean against him. "Then get me something to wear," I order him.

Jax laughs. "Yes, I think I'm going to enjoy you a lot." He turns to his trunk and drops the wand in. He pulls off his own silk jacket and wraps it around my shoulders, buttoning the front. The backs of his hands brush across my breasts and they perk up. I have to fight against inhaling sharply. I've never felt like this before, but I want more of it. I want to go wherever this man goes. I want to keep feeling this way.

"I think I'll keep you for a while," he says. He opens the back of the car, but this time when I get in, he doesn't tie me down.

I think this might be progress for both of us.

11

JAX

Who is this girl?

I drive most of the night. I watch her in the backseat. After about an hour, she lies down and falls asleep. Her hair is wild and tangled around her face.

Something tickles in my belly, something annoying, something like interest. I force it away and focus on the task at hand. I can't just waltz into a Vigilante silo with a naked woman in bondage rope. If her information is wiped, no telling who she is.

I refuse to allow any thought that she might actually be innocent.

Ordinary people have Identipad entries that are pages long. Social media accounts. Addresses. Records. I can see every filling in their teeth and every bad grade on their high school transcript. There is nothing the Vigilantes haven't compiled on every citizen of every country. People make it too easy with their long digital trails, interconnected with everyone they know and every place they've been.

But Mia is blank. Her parents too.

Then I realize, so is my family.

When they left the network, retired, their identities were erased. It's a courtesy.

But this girl. She's a working girl. She was in a safe house.

I rub my eyes. Nothing should be hidden from me. Before Jovana and my prison sentence, I was next in line to take over the entire North American syndicate. That would include this beautiful girl and her aunt's Tennessee home. I should know them. Be able to see their histories, functions, and allies. Even if they are wiped. Even if they have special classification.

And yet, I can't.

They could be transplants from another syndicate. Russian, maybe. Or someplace small. Norway. Mia's features are very delicate. Her hair is a mix of brown and gold.

Damn it, who is she?

The lights of St. Louis become visible in the distance. We'll be in the city soon. I'll need to decide what to do with the girl. Dump her? Lock her away?

But if I bring her to the silo, I might learn more about her. Standard procedure at every Vigilante station is a complete rundown of recent activity, biomedical, geolocation, technology use. Everything. You couldn't give a blow job without it being on the screen as you walked through the glass hall.

It would tell me about her.

I punch the screen on the dash to activate the search function. "Find me a five-star hotel," I say softly, to avoid waking Mia.

A list appears. Ritz-Carlton. Four Seasons. Cheshire. Moonrise.

"Ritz," I say.

A gentle female voice says, "The Club Level Executive Suite is available."

"Take it," I say.

"Reserving it now."

I will need to provide something for Mia to wear to the silo. I swipe away the hotel screen. No traditional boutiques are open at this hour. I glance back at her. The jacket has slipped and I can see the swell of her breasts crossed by the red rope. Something stirs again.

"Fetish boutique," I say to the screen.

But the list is totally unsatisfactory. Bondage shops. Cheap adult stores. St. Louis hides the good stuff.

Who would know where to find a service to provide couture clothes to a girl who is tied up? Someone discreet who wouldn't blink at the ropes?

"Contact Armond," I say.

"Contacting," the voice responds.

After a moment, Armond pops up on the video screen. His bald head shines blue from whatever lighting he's under. His eyes are bright under bushy brows. "Jax! You're back on grid!"

"Not exactly," I say.

Armond glances down. "I see. Now that's what I call encryption. It says I'm in Buenos Aires."

"And I'm in Tahiti," I say. "I need a favor."

"Anything, my friend."

He doesn't even ask why I'm out of prison. Some things you don't say even on encrypted channels.

"I need something lovely, size four, daywear, think high-class secretary."

Armond guffaws a loud laugh. "You're more like a size ten, I'd say."

I shake my head. "Right. I do drag about like you do mezcal."

Armond's expression shifts to disgust. "Do not speak of it." He's from Jalisco and his tequilas are pure blue agave always. We've tossed a few back more than once.

"Also, we have a little bondage involved," I say. "So send me someone prepared to handle role-play."

He taps on something below his screen. "I need some coordinates."

"Remember when we found six hookers in a meth lab?"

"Can't forget that one."

"The tall one. Her name. My usual spot. Usual suite."

"Roger that," he says. "I'll send a couple ladies expecting to outfit a boss and secretary bondage game."

"Perfect," I say. Armond is the expert at these things.

"I'm not seeing that gray suit I sent your French compatriot," he says.

"I should have known that was you." I jerk my head toward the back. "The lady has the jacket."

He nods knowingly. "Understood. Shoe size?"

I glance to the backseat. Mia's slender foot is tucked under her knee, the Croc about to fall off. "I'd guess a seven."

"All right. It will be ready for you when you arrive. ETA?"

I glance at the map still projected on the lower dash. "A little less than an hour."

"We'll get it done."

"Thank you, Armond."

"It's a pleasure, as always." He nods and the screen blips out.

"Six hookers?" Mia's voice is full of sleep.

"It's code," I say, even though that one isn't.

She sits up, her hair falling around her shoulders like a cloud. Damn, she's sexy. The innocence paired with the attitude. I've never met anyone like her.

"We're almost to the city," I say. "I have reserved a hotel."

She glances down at the suit jacket and frowns at how much she's revealing. "I don't think they're going to approve of my walking through the lobby in red rope and a man's jacket."

"I have my own entrance," I say.

"Of course," she mutters. She shakes her head, trying to get her hair to fall back. "Am I going to be tied up like this for long?"

I set the car back into controlled drive and turn to look at her. The suit jacket splits at her thighs, pale and slender on the black leather seat. Her knees are pressed tightly together. She wears no makeup, so nothing about her is smudged or used up. Other than the wild tangle of her hair, she's like an angel. The urge to unbutton the jacket and look at her again is powerful. It's the dry spell, I tell myself. I never fall for Phase One seductress Trainees.

When I raise my eyes to hers, I feel like she knows the direction of my thoughts. As if the innocent act is gone completely and she knows what I want. I wait for those knees to part, for her to open wide in invitation, her chest arching toward me.

But she just shifts on the seat, fighting against the ties on her wrists so that she's less uncomfortable.

"How long you're tied up depends on how well you cooperate," I say and turn around, both for her sake and mine.

I need to be back under control again, and this girl is not helping.

12

MIA

This must be how celebrities do it.

Jax pulls the car up to some strange little back entrance to the hotel. It has a tiny covered canopy and a doorman who must get an eyeful of all sorts of rich and famous people.

The doors are whisked open and nobody blinks an eye at me in my suit jacket with the red ropes trailing from the back. In fact, I think I may have caught the doorman winking at Jax!

Unbelievable.

Jax told me as we arrived at the Ritz-Carlton that if I promised not to scream or yell, he wouldn't gag me. Rich men bringing in beautiful women dressed as fetish girls in bondage was common and nobody would pay attention to my insisting I was kidnapped.

I am not sure I believe him, but being seen in this getup is humiliating enough. So I agree to go without a gag. Besides, Jax put some Band-Aid-looking device on my throat that he claims will warn him if I am about to scream. It will give him time to do something. What that might be, he doesn't say.

So here I am, passing through some secret door and immediately getting turned down a silent hall and up a small elevator. Within seconds, a white door with a gold handle is opened wide, and I'm ushered into the poshest hotel room that quite possibly has ever existed.

I'm dumbstruck. There's a fountain. A fountain in the middle of a hotel room.

White sofas face big French windows. The curtains are gold. There are fresh flowers in vases on every surface. An enormous marble fireplace contains a crackling log.

I step farther inside. Jax drops the red rope and it trails behind me out the bottom of the suit jacket. I walk across the soft carpet and spot doors to the bedroom. I halt instantly. I'm not going in there.

But then I see another door leading to a bathroom with a garden tub and two toilets. Really? Two? This, I head straight for.

It's only when I actually arrive beside the porcelain seat that I realize my hands are behind me, tied, and I can't do anything with my panties. Still, I have to pee so badly that I'm determined to make it work. I start wriggling back and forth, trying to get my underwear down.

Jax comes in the doorway and leans on the frame, an amused quirk of a smile on his face. "Need some help?"

I stomp to the door and shove it closed with my shoulder, but he catches the bottom with his foot. "We have visitors," he says. "They may be of assistance."

He points through a second door to the bedroom, where two ladies are sitting in a pair of fancy chairs. Beside them is a large trunk, open wide, an array of dresses and pants and sweaters on display.

"Who are they?" I whisper.

"They are here to attend to you," he says. "They think I'm outfitting you for a bit of boss and secretary bondage role-play."

I kick at him, but he deftly dodges my poorly aimed Croc.

"She's a feisty one," he tells the women.

They smile and nod. Both are dark skinned and beautiful with perfect hair, wearing classy tailored pantsuits with clever scarves.

One of them stands and approaches the door. "I'm Emma," she says. "Would you like a bath?"

Actually, after the strip-down in the middle of a hayfield, that sounds like heaven. I whip my hips to one side to reveal the long tail of my red ropes. "I'm a little tied up for that," I say.

Emma glances over at Jax. "Should we untie her for the bath?"

He turns to me. "I will do it."

I take a step back. "Never mind," I say. "I just need to pee."

Emma enters the bathroom and closes the door on Jax. This, he allows.

She turns to me. "I'll help." Her expression never shifts. A total professional. I wonder what sort of craziness she sees on a daily basis.

Emma lifts the lid to one of the toilets, and I realize the other one doesn't have a cover at all. It's different, with a funny gold button on the side. I stare at it, craning my head to figure out what it does.

"It's a bidet," Emma says. "Have you not seen one before?"

I shake my head.

She smiles to herself. I hate that I feel like a country bumpkin in front of strangers. Jax is bad enough.

I've never peed in front of anyone, but apparently I'm going to today. I step over to the toilet, and Emma bends to peel down my underwear. "At least you aren't tied up down there!" she says.

Small mercies, I guess. I sit down and realize the seat is actually warm. Crazy.

Emma turns and fusses with towels on a rack, so I have a small bit of privacy. I wonder how to approach her, let her know I've been kidnapped. My brave moment in the field has long passed now, and I want to go home. Jax is so confusing, maddening.

This little fiasco has gotten embarrassing. And now he's brought in witnesses.

"Have you worked with Jax before?" I ask.

She gives a little shrug and sets to arranging bottles of shampoo on the edge of the tub. Oh, the luxury of a bath.

Maybe I can escape without telling her anything. "All this role-play is sort of silly. Do you think you could untie me for a bath?" I ask. "I would love one."

"No, ma'am. Not without Jax's say."

Damn. I start to stand and realize I can't even wipe. Good grief.

But with all the simple proficiency of a hospital nurse, Emma takes a handful of toilet paper, pats me dry, and flushes the toilet.

I close my eyes as she wriggles my panties back into place, trying to reconcile my current life with the one I was leading just a few hours ago. It doesn't line up. All I can picture is my mother, her wild carefree expression. Be like her, I remind myself. Have courage.

When I open my eyes again, Emma is patiently waiting. "I think you will like our selections for you," she says.

Clothes. Now that's an improvement. I can feel the ropes chafing my skin along my ribs.

I follow her through the bedroom door. The other woman has spread several outfits on the bed. Jax is not in the room. We're alone.

I decide to just go for it.

"I've been kidnapped," I say quickly. "Please, call the police. My name is Mia Morrow."

The women look at each other and back at me.

"We understand," Emma says. "We will make sure the police are on their way."

Then the two of them murmur together over which scarf to put with a navy blue pant set.

"Are you listening?" I say in a forced whisper. "Jax took me from my home! I live in Tennessee."

They glance up, smile, and sort through a small box of underwear. Emma holds up a red thong and the other nods her approval.

Jax appears in the doorway, a drink in his hand. "Everything all right?" he asks.

"Just fine, Mr. De Luca," Emma says. "Your lady was just telling us to call the police."

I want to stomp my foot. Oh, those hussies!

He steps in the room. "Did she now?" He saunters up to me. "I might have to punish you for that. Shall I spank you?"

The women pinch their lips together to hide their smiles.

Oh, God.

Jax toys with the button of the jacket as if he might unfasten it. "I've missed seeing these," he says, as if we were longtime lovers. "Shall I send the ladies away?"

"No!" I say quickly. "We were looking for outfits."

He takes a sip of the drink. I can smell the liquor, lush and expensive. My eyes fix on the amber liquid surrounding perfect cubes of ice.

Jax holds it out. "Would you like a sip?"

"I don't drink," I say.

He nods approvingly. "I like my secretaries sober," he says. "Except, maybe, for now." He presses the cold glass against my lips. "Just a little taste."

He tilts the glass, and I gulp to avoid the drink spilling down my chin. It's pure fire going down, just a trace of something bitter, then a hint of something sweet.

I swallow, feeling it burn all the way to my belly. The warmth quickly spreads throughout my entire body.

"What was that?" I ask.

He holds up the glass to the light. "An Old Fashioned," he says. "Like me."

"Hardly," I say. I shift my arm to wipe my lips, forgetting my hands are tied.

Jax notices and lifts his thumb to my mouth. "You missed some," he says huskily. He brushes a finger across my lips, then brings it to his tongue. "You taste delicious."

My heart beats ninety to nothing. I'm torn between the old Mia, full of panic and fear, and my mother's Mia, courageous and strong. Will this man hurt me? Or will he take me to some new amazing place?

I already regret trying to have the women call the police. I want him. It's hard to accept. But I do.

"I'd like to see her in one of your outfits," he says to Emma. "You may untie her."

Before I can say anything, Emma unbuttons Jax's jacket and pulls it away. My breath catches as Jax's eyes linger on my body once more, the red ropes, my breasts. My breathing speeds up.

The two women begin working the ties. I sigh in relief as Emma releases my wrists.

Jax sips his drink, watching with an intensity I've never known. I don't know what to do. I feel crazy with need. The ropes drop to the floor.

"You have some other panties for her?" he asks.

"Of course," Emma says. "Shall we take these away?"

I suck in a breath. No one has ever seen me naked. But my nipples tighten, and a hot buzz zips through me like an electric shock.

The feeling is overwhelming. Jax's fingers twitch by his thigh as if they want to reach out for me, remove my last scrap of clothing himself.

I feel lost. I don't know what I want more. For him to leave, or for him to keep appraising me the way he is now, like a wolf about to devour its prey. My skin hums with awareness.

"She's beautiful, isn't she?" he says to the women, who nod in agreement.

Emma slips my plain panties down my thighs. Jax sniffs, as if covering some other sound. He's hiding his desire. I can feel it. I feel a surge of power again. This man wants me.

Nobody has ever wanted me.

The feeling is intense, more intoxicating than

his drink. More addictive than his letters.

I think back for a moment to those words on those sheaves of paper. They started this whole thing. Why had I written him back? Somewhere in my mind, had I wanted this exact thing? A dangerous prisoner to escape, to take me, to sweep me away?

I was getting exactly what I asked for.

"Bring her out when she's dressed," he says, as if he can take no more. He turns back to the main room.

I don't want him to leave. Not yet. "Hey," I say. "Can I have that bath?"

He looks back, assessing me, and my body bursts with need. God, it's like a drug. I want him to keep staring, to keep wanting. I've never felt so powerful.

His crisp white shirt is unbuttoned at the neck, and I can see his Adam's apple working in his throat. "Yes," he says and turns to Emma. "Give us a moment."

The women hurry away to prepare the bath. When they are out of sight, he walks up very close to me. The thrumming in my body reaches a fever pitch. I don't have on a stitch of clothing. The room is softly lit with lamps on either side of the bed. A more seductive scene never existed.

He's only inches away. His finger touches me just beneath my chin. "You're better than I thought," he says.

I have to swallow hard to get any words out. "What do you mean?"

His hand moves to the small of my back and presses flat against my skin. He pulls me against his hips, and I understand what he's talking about when I feel the hard bulge press against my belly.

"Some things you inspire without even trying," he says.

I can barely breathe. We're connected, the soft fabric of his pants luxurious against my stomach. His hand is warm and firm on my naked back.

"Damn, you are beautiful," he says. His lips are inches from mine. I can almost taste him, the Old Fashioned probably still lingering on his tongue.

I'm on fire. Neither of us moves. I'm caught between fear and fierce desire.

His letters flash through me, all those words, the heat I felt all these months, reading about his intoxicating need. And now it is right here, hot and hard against my actual body.

His jaw is scruffy with stubble. I resist the urge to reach up and touch it. I want something to happen, but I don't know what. A kiss, maybe. Just that. I have another chance, right here. He's close enough.

Am I brave enough to do it? I stare at his mouth. My breathing has gotten shallow.

Jax shifts, just slightly, the smallest increment closer to me. The bulge between us fits against me a little tighter. I suck in a breath.

The finger beneath my chin moves down, caressing my throat. This is it, I think. He's going to do it. He'll kiss me. Something will happen. Will I take it all the way? How far can I go? The pulsing need in my body tells me I won't stop him from anything he wants to do to me.

But he rests his finger on the small device he has applied to my neck. "Enjoy your bath," he says. "But know this has a sedative. Don't run or do anything sudden, or you will set it off. You'll be out cold in seconds."

I pull back from him, breaking our connection. My hand goes to my throat, feeling for the adhesive.

Jax steps away. "I wouldn't touch it. It

activates if you try to pull it off, like one of those security devices in clothing stores."

I jerk my fingers from my neck. I'm ready to spit fire. He's toying with me. Acting like he's caught by me, just so he can push me away again.

I hate him. Fury blasts through me.

"Get out of here," I say. "I need some time without you staring at me like a lecherous beast."

He bows from the waist. "As you wish, fair Mia." His eyes graze my body one more time, then he disappears into the other room.

My body goes cold instantly. I spot a robe hanging on a hook and snatch it up, holding it in front of me. I'm shaky and mad and disappointed and disgusted with myself. Lolling around a hotel room naked like a common trollop, hoping some jerk pays attention to me.

I want to weep into the soft terrycloth, but I won't. I'm not that Mia anymore. I'm going to get through this. I am strong.

Emma steps out of the bathroom. "You ready?"

I walk toward the garden tub, roiling with a million conflicting emotions. I'm not afraid of Jax. And I've given up on being shy. But I don't know what I want. I try to imagine myself back in my aunt's house, puttering around in solitude, and I can't see it.

But this Jax. He's so hard to understand. And I don't know what he wants from me.

Or what I want from him.

13

Jax

Sometime in the morning hours, I jerk instantly awake. Every muscle tenses and prepares for battle, a skill drilled into me in my youth. I assess my surroundings to make sure nothing has changed, that there are no intruders.

Darkness blankets the hotel suite. No sounds. I flip my wrist and press a button on the knife holster, which scans for thermal shifts. Only the fireplace coals show as red. I'm alone in the room.

A thud from above lets me know this is what awakened me. I'm disgruntled that this suite is not on the top floor. Noises from above always bring me fully awake in seconds.

I switch on a lamp. The dim face of a clock reads five a.m. Might as well begin the day. Laid out on the easy chair is a suit bag, left by the two women last night. A quick peek inside confirms the contents: a clean undershirt, soft cotton boxers, socks. And a killer charcoal suit with impeccable tailoring.

Armond, you're a godsend.

I cast my shirt and pants aside and go through my daily exercises in my boxers, still the rough prison variety left from my escape.

Sit-ups, push-ups, some simple yoga stretches, and a round of tai chi. It feels good to do them somewhere other than a concrete cell. Workout complete, I head into the bathroom by the outer door, stifling the urge to go into the bedroom.

I shower and dress in the clean suit, then brace myself to check on Mia. No telling what sort of mood she'll be in today. When the two women left, they said she was clean and dressed and ready for me to approve her outfit, but I decided to let them make the choices. I left her alone.

Chicken, my gut tells me. But I prefer to think of it as careful. Something is happening with her that suggests different training than I would expect from her at age twenty.

Most Vigilante girls finish college before going into service, but other families place their daughters in the program in their teens. Only a few will put younger children in training, although cunning youth are very useful in certain situations.

The Vigilante life is a birthright, but you still have to choose it. When my parents informed me at age twelve of my position, I went straight into boot camp, excited by the possibilities. My older brother Arthur, however, being scientifically minded and desiring a career marked by test tubes and Bunsen burners, opted out.

It's been a good life, even though my parents left the program when I turned thirty.

Or at least it *was* good, until this past year and my imprisonment.

I assess my scruffy face in the bathroom mirror. I'm not sure what Mia sees when she looks at me. Her kidnapper, no doubt. But she is such a case in opposites. Frightened, then brave. Angry, then cunning. Innocent, then seductively standing naked by a bed.

Who is this girl I have taken into my possession? I'm not sure if I should be protecting her or keeping up my own guard.

I have concerns about entering a high-security silo. There might be hostility. If they do finally arrange a tribunal to hear the facts surrounding my murder of another Vigilante, it could take days. I probably should leave the girl out of it.

But if I enter the facility, I will learn more about Mia's past.

I want to know who she is, where she comes from, what the Vigilantes plan to do with her. She should have a career path, a training regimen. Maybe I can influence it, or at least know where she is.

Unless she's an enemy. In that case, she can rot along with Jovana and her ilk.

I open the bedroom door carefully, quietly.

Mia sleeps soundly in the bed. The red ropes loosely hold her in place, tied by the two women per my instructions. The knots are rough and unpracticed, but they do their job.

Mia's honey-brown hair spills over the fluffy

pillows like strands of fine silk. Even though her arms are tied, she has managed to pin the covers with her elbows. The sheet is pulled to her chin, but I spy the strap of a red negligee.

Armond must have sent word of my favorite color. Against her pale skin, the swath of crimson stands out like a warning flag.

As it should. The last time I inspected a woman this closely, she got me sent to prison.

Mia stirs as I cross the room. Her eyes flutter for a second before awareness hits and she wakes with a gasp.

"Good morning, temptress," I say.

She stares at me and pulls against her bonds. A grimace creases her brow.

"Are you going to let me up?" she asks. "This isn't exactly comfortable." Her words carry a hint of accusation.

"In a moment. First, we talk."

She looks down for a moment as if to ensure her modesty, then lets her gaze slide back my way.

"I am going to a Vigilante stronghold. There I hope to find out where Klaus might be and start the process of clearing my name."

Her eyes shine with some thought. Hope of

being left behind, alone?

"You are coming with me," I add with a smile.

"Why?" The shine is gone.

"Because I need you. And I'm curious. The Vigilantes have info on everyone. Everyone except you. If I can't find the answers I seek at the silo, I will extract information from you. I can make you talk."

Mia visibly swallows. She probably thinks I'm talking about torture. Poor girl.

"Don't worry, Mia. I like you, remember?"

"Parts of you do," she says blandly.

Now she is behaving more like I expected.

I approach the bed. Mia stiffens a little, which makes me smile. Back to her training. The frightened act.

I know better. She stood naked before me last night and waited for me to kiss her. I didn't give her the satisfaction, although I sorely could have used it myself.

I pull out the first knot in the ropes binding her to the bed. She drops the scared expression and stretches her arm. Her sigh of contentment goes straight to my gut.

I feel that hitch, that pull of desire. I quash it

with a quick spike of anger.

"Do not think for an instant that I will hesitate to do what it takes to keep you in line," I say. I tug on the rope for emphasis.

"Hey!" she says with a glare. She shifts on the bed and the sheet slips down to reveal the fiery lace negligee. It cups her breasts, pushing them into an impossibly deep cleavage, then falls in a sheer swath of red to where she is hidden again by the covers.

Is she playing with me? I trust her even less than I did a moment ago. Still, my body's reaction is swift. I want her. I have to clamp down on my jaw to resist the urge to press her down on the bed and end this charade right now.

"Up," I say.

She jerks against the rope. "How?" A flash of anger makes her face even more beautiful.

"Fine." I untie everything except the binds around each of her wrists.

"Hand me that dress," she says. "And the bra."

I intend to make another searing remark. But instead, I turn to the red sweater dress draped over the side chair. Next to it, a small box holds a matching bra.

I pass her the clothing, and she pulls it beneath the covers and disappears under a bulge of blanket.

After a moment, the red negligee flies through the air. It hits the beige carpet like a bloodstain.

I lean against the wall, my anger dissipating. I've never seen a woman act like this. Temptress, then shy girl. It's entertaining, at least.

Mia slides from the covers fully dressed, but the sweater hugs her curves in all the best places as she moves toward the bathroom.

She insists on closing the door, pointing to the device on her neck. I nod.

It doesn't matter. There's no way a half-trained Phase One can escape me, and I'm done playing games about it. There is no window in the bathroom. If she exited either door, I could drop her unconscious in seconds.

I head to the main room and pull out the Vigilante tech kit Sam gave me. I pick up my watch and check the band. With just the right motion, two short, sharp prongs slip out. The tips glisten with contact poison. Handy.

The bathroom door opens and Mia emerges, looking rather resplendent despite her disheveled hair. The dress gives with every motion and seems to ripple over her body. She moves with an inborn grace.

Mia holds out her arms where the long trail of ropes are looped around her delicate wrists. "Ready to lead me out of here like a slave girl?"

I approach and her surprise is palpable as I untie her wrists and free her fully from her binding.

"Why didn't you do that earlier?" she asks as she rubs the marks on her skin. "Would have made things easier." She glances back into the bathroom.

I chuckle. "It would have, yes. But where's the fun in that?"

"You're an ass," she says.

For a moment, camaraderie courses between us, like we're on the same team.

But we're not. I can't forget that. Not for an instant.

"We will be walking out of here together." I let my voice go cold. "Remember that I can sedate you at any time, so I suggest you behave yourself. A woman fainting won't raise an eyebrow from the staff."

She frowns, the easy teasing gone. It's best that we both remember our place in this scheme.

"I need my shoes," she says.

I wave in the direction of the bedroom. Mia heads there, looking confused and torn. I have an urge to touch her, give her some sort of comfort. Damn, this girl is vexing.

I'm starting to sense that maybe she had juvenile training early on and this faltering temptress trick is something new. Still, shoddy work. I feel increasingly certain that she's part of Jovana's brood, and not true Vigilante. The program is unsurpassed in matching a trainee with his or her natural gifts, and they would never place a half-prepared Vigilante in a safe house.

Mia comes back, teetering unsteadily on stiletto heels. "This is a new look for me," she says.

Great. She'll be incapable of walking more than five feet. No matter. We have to get moving.

I touch a button on the table and within minutes, a man enters. With only a faint nod from me, he gathers my packed suit and another red bag that contains additional outfits for Mia.

When he has gone out ahead of us, I say, "It's time."

She has walked to the French doors and turns, backlit by the morning sun. Her hair is glorious and wild, the red dress giving her a sultry silhouette.

Yes, she will make one hell of an operative, in time.

I step forward and take her hand. She makes an obvious show of looking away but does not resist.

We walk the hotel hallway in silence. Mia concentrates on her balance as we go down the elevator and arrive at the back entrance.

The Lexus is already waiting in the pull-through, the driver's door hanging open. The attendant opens the front passenger door, and Mia hesitates for a second before climbing in. I slip into the driver's seat and pull away the moment he closes her door.

I'm not sure how much I should warn her about what we're about to go into. If she's a Vigilante, she's been to syndicates before.

I consider the possibility that Mia's information board will be as blank at the silo as it was on the Identipad. If that's true, I'll ask them to hold on to her for me. I'll get to the bottom of who she is on my own.

If she really is one of my enemies, she'll be captured. I'll take great pleasure in interrogating her myself, no holds barred.

Great pleasure.

Mia stares out the window, lost in thought. Her

skin is fair in the morning light. I may just have to accept the fact that I'm caught by her.

I decide not to say anything about the situation. Hopefully things will work out without too much drama. I'll go in, confess my role in killing Jovana's rival and how it came about, and we'll start the process of clearing my name.

After the night it all went down, no one brought me to the syndicate for questioning. I was taken to Ridley Prison like a common criminal, without any sort of Vigilante tribunal. I aim to find out who arranged that and why no one stepped forward to challenge how my case was handled.

"Is it far?" Mia asks.

"An hour," I say.

Mia smooths out a rumple in her skirt. She seems almost nervous. I wonder if she has something to hide, something that will be revealed when she enters the silo. Maybe she plans to attack me and escape before we arrive.

This is going to be a very interesting morning.

14

MIA

Jax seems different than last night.

I steal peeks at him as he drives. This car, now that I'm in the front, isn't like anything I've ever seen. The dash at first glance seems like the new fancy electrics. A whole-car perimeter camera screen. Gauges that tell you time to next charge, miles per amp, the size of your environmental footprint.

But there's other things. Maps display on the

windshield. There's a countdown that is twenty-four hours in and will end in forty-eight more.

Another inexplicable hexagon projected onto the glass has pulsing red lights of varying brightness.

"So what is that one?" I ask, curiosity eating at me. I point to the hexagon.

Jax shifts his attention to the display. In the bright light of day, he seems less imposing. His eyes are actually a gray-blue, now that I can see them beneath his hooded brow.

He's ridiculously handsome. I've never seen anyone like him before. Maybe in a movie.

I remember him looking at me last night, when I thought he would kiss me. My heart quickens.

"That is just a view of my compatriots and their positions," he says. The way his voice dips on the word "compatriots" suggests that the dots represent something quite the opposite of anything friendly.

"You said my aunt's house was 'compromised' last night. How, exactly?"

His eyes flick over to me, then go back to the road. "It was your own alarm that went off. You should know."

"I had no idea there was anything in my lampshade."

His expression darkens. That's the Jax I remember. Angry. Suspicious. I've hit a nerve.

"It should have been updated with a more current model. Did you only recently go to that safe house?"

This question feels like a trick. He knows how long I have been writing the letters.

"I grew up there. I was gone for a couple years to community college. I came back to care for my aunt."

His face gets even more sullen. He thinks I'm lying, but I don't get why. How can he assume that I know anything? I suddenly understand how innocent people are convicted of crimes. It doesn't matter that you have nothing to do with it. You're guilty just by being at the wrong place at the wrong time.

"I'm not sure why you feel it necessary to lie to me," he says. "I'm a high-ranking Vigilante. I know everything about that house."

"I don't think you do," I protest. "You say someone named Georgiana Powers lived there, but that can't possibly be true. My Aunt Bea has owned it for decades. I lived there for most of my childhood. You're wrong." I shake my head. "You're just too stubborn to say you're wrong."

"I'm never wrong," he says. "That's how I've gotten where I am."

I snort out the most unladylike sound. "Ridley Prison? Am I supposed to believe that is some sort of exalted position?" I turn away from him to stare at the majestic pine trees stacked deep along the highway. We must be driving alongside some sort of national park, because the road narrows and there are no longer any houses or businesses.

He stews in silence, but I don't care. I'm only stating the obvious. I have nothing to lose here. I've accepted all the things that could happen. Abduction. Rape. Torture. Okay, not the torture. I can't accept that. If they kill me, I can only hope it will be quick.

I just can't imagine why I could possibly be worth this much trouble.

"Is it the letters?" I ask, turning back to him. I hope I sound as contrite as I feel.

He concentrates on the road. "What do you mean?"

"The reason you kidnapped me. Is it because I

pretended to be Klaus?" I swallow hard over the lump in my throat. "I'm truly sorry. I just thought your letters were…intriguing and that it wouldn't hurt anything to answer them. I thought you enjoyed them."

A muscle twitches in his jaw. I'm somehow making him more angry with my bumbling apology.

"Just stop it now," he says. "There is no way you are not involved. Even if your poorly executed letters are just ramblings, you were still at a Vigilante safe house that was the last known location of my friend and comrade."

I give up. He won't listen to me. He thinks everything I say is a lie. We're driving to some place I can't even fathom, but if it's like this car, like the gadgets in his trunk or the training he seems to have, then it's bound to be dangerous.

My belly flips a little. I realize we haven't eaten and he hasn't even thought of it. Maybe this Vigilante runs on anger and the misery of others. I probably couldn't swallow anything anyway.

As if he's read my mind, he says, "It's too risky to stop for breakfast along this route. They'll provide for you at the syndicate."

"No room service at the Ritz?" I tease.

"I got poisoned twice at hotels," he says grimly. "Security is far too lax."

This shuts me up. What sort of life gets you poisoned at a fancy hotel? And what sort of man survives it — twice?

We turn off the highway onto a gravel road. The trees tower on either side of our car and soon we're surrounded by woods.

I have to stuff down my rising fear. This looks like a very good place to leave a body. I wonder if Jax could do that, if he could kill me. Everything about him tells me it's possible.

Except, last night. That almost-kiss. He feels something, same as me. I press my hand against my quivering belly. The sweater dress is soft and smooth. Cashmere, Emma said last night. Only the best for me, she said. I was lucky.

Lucky. Ha.

The road gets more bumpy, and even in this expensive car, we start lurching in our seats. Jax keeps both hands on the wheel and stares straight ahead.

The hexagon lights up with red dots, bright and pulsing brightly. They are concentrated on a space we seem to be approaching.

With a jerk of the wheel, Jax steers us into the woods. Underbrush crunches beneath the tires, and small trees are mowed down. After a few yards, we come to a stop beneath a canopy of trees.

"Why did you drive off the road?" I ask.

"We can't just cruise right up to the door," he says. "If things don't go well, I want to have a vehicle."

"They don't know you just drove up in this thing?"

"We're outside the high-surveillance perimeter and hidden from satellites by the trees. Besides, the car is cloaked. Even if they come across it, the identity attached to it is civilian. They'll assume an accident."

I realize I'm gripping the door handle so hard my fingers hurt. "So we walk the rest of the way?" I ask.

He glances down at my shoes. "You have any others?" he asks.

"I can look." I turn around in my seat, reaching through the car to my red bag in the back.

I dig for a second, and the red bondage rope spills out. I shake my head at the memory. Unfortunately, the only other shoes in the bag are a pair of knee boots on platforms.

I turn back to Jax. "The boots are worse. Boss and secretary role-play outfits don't come with a practical side."

"What happened to those shoes you brought from home?"

I feel around in the bag. "I guess I left them at the hotel." Along with that red nightie the women put me in.

He taps the steering wheel in agitation. "It isn't far, but the terrain might be difficult."

"I'll manage," I say. And I will. If there's anything I'm good at, it's soldiering through.

"We're going to walk up the main path," he says and opens his door. "I'd appreciate it if you don't mention the car to anyone once we're inside."

I pop open the handle and place a tentative foot outside in the dirt and pinecones.

Jax comes around. I keep my knees tightly together as I twist in my seat and prepare to stand in these heels on the uneven ground.

He holds out his hand. I hesitate, then place my fingers on his. He grasps me firmly. I stand uncertainly, the tiny point of the shoes snapping through twigs and leaves.

The minute I put my weight on my heels, though, I sink at least three inches, falling back into the car.

"Well," Jax says. "This is going to be interesting." He pulls me back to standing.

I take care to keep my weight in my toes this time.

He seems to be controlling his patience. I hang on to his hand and take a tentative step. Walking on my toes works much better, and by the time I'm away from the car and the door is closed, I have a handle on my balance on the broken ground.

"I need to get some things from the trunk," he says. He lets go of my hand.

I stand in the woods. "At least they don't know we're here yet," I say.

"Of course they do," he says, his voice tight. "The minute we got out of the car, they had our heat signatures." He lifts the trunk. "I have maybe thirty seconds to choose my weapons and get away from this vehicle so it can stay cloaked." He glances at me, still wobbling a bit in the shoes. "If you don't wreck the whole plan."

"Me! Wreck your plan! This ridiculous idea to waltz into some high-security silo-whatever even though those same people just stuck you in prison?"

Jax ignores me, sorting through his things.

Oh, that man is infuriating.

Hot. Sexy. Impressive.

But infuriating.

15

JAX

Life is nothing but a ticking clock lately.

I open the trunk to rapidly sort through all the tools at my disposal. I hadn't anticipated the complication of Mia's wardrobe malfunctions when I planned to get us away from the car before our identities might be tied to it.

We can't stay near a cloaked device too long or someone will send a bot for a visual, and the car is obviously here. It's only invisible to heat sensors and signals, which the Vigilantes rely on at this range. Even with the fake ID on the car, the two of us hovering near it will give it away.

I pick up what looks like a thick piece of cellophane with a black band along one edge. My fingers graze the surface and several icons light up. It's the latest model of an electronic skeleton key. Sam was still working out the bugs in the prototype when I entered prison. Looks like he finished it while I was gone. Hopefully. I slip it into a hidden pocket in the lining of my jacket.

Next I put a tiny, delicate bit of filament in my ear. On its own it acts as a short-range hearing enhancement device, but paired to my Blackphone it can act as a remote earpiece and radio scanner.

I carefully check the knife sheath along my arm. It's highly unlikely they'll let me keep it, but it is an acceptable weapon inside a silo for a Vigilante.

"Let's go," I say and close the trunk.

Mia follows without a word. I maneuver her in front of me to keep an eye on both her and our path to the silo.

When we're a decent distance from the car, I punch a button on the key chain and one of the tires deflates.

Mia gasps. "What did you do that for?"

"To make it appear as though a normal civilian has left it due to a flat."

"Ohhhh. So they won't take it."

"Exactly."

"But how will we get away?"

I click the button a second time, and the tire inflates instantly.

"I need one of those," she says.

I deflate the tire once more. While Mia stares at her shoes, I toss the key chain in a tree. Can't have them confiscating that.

Mia takes an uncertain step. "Is it far?" she asks, snatching at my hand as she makes her first hard stumble in the underbrush.

"A bit."

She starts getting her footing better as we walk. She's doing much better by the time we make the turn toward the silo entrance, and the gravel is replaced by an empty stretch of asphalt.

"Wow," she says, slowing down to look.

The silo is buried in the side of a low hill, almost entirely concrete. It housed missiles during the Cold War, but once it was abandoned, like many of the silos all over the world, the Vigilantes staked their claim to it. These shared spaces are part of the few tenuous links between the traditional governments of the various nations and the Vigilante network.

We approach the looming concrete walls that flank an enormous set of metal doors. The exterior appears abandoned, choked with brush and silted with layers of dirt.

We are still fifty yards out when the doors slide open. The leaves flutter as a whoosh of air exits the facility. Mia halts, out of fear, possibly. Or ready to run. I grasp her hand tightly. She won't escape me now.

Two men step from the door. One is dressed in a brown blazer over blue jeans. His walk is focused but unhurried, someone who knows the drill.

The other wears running skins and a body-hugging long-sleeved top. His cut muscles are discernible even from this distance, and his posture speaks of arrogance.

They wait for us to approach. Neither openly carries a weapon, but I have no doubt they are both armed. I'm sure Running Man thinks himself a master martial artist as well. I pay him little mind. It's obvious that Mr. Blazer outranks him. When we're about five yards away, Mr. Blazer calls out.

"Jax De Luca," he says. "You and your companion will come with us for security screening. If you have any weapons, please display them now. Failure to comply will be seen as hostile intent, and we will respond with force."

Running Man purses his lips and shakes his hands to the side as if loosening up. He reminds me of a cocky cage fighter before he gets his face pummeled by an overpowering opponent.

I would never be so foolish as to bring a substantial weapon to a silo. I flick my wrist, activating the holster to drop the knife into my palm. It winks in the sun as I hold it up.

Mia lets go of my hand. "You brought a knife!" she hisses.

"All right," says Mr. Blazer. "Come with us. Please keep the knife in view."

Mia huffs in surprise that they allow me to keep the blade. This makes me wonder if she's been in a silo after all. It's impossible to be Vigilante trained without living in one for a time. She should know the basic rules.

Mr. Blazer turns and walks back to the entrance without looking to see if we follow.

Running Man gives me a small sneer as we pass. I raise an eyebrow and give him a mocking smirk in reply. I can feel his eyes boring into my back as he falls in behind us.

"You seem to have me at a disadvantage in names, Mr....?" I ask Mr. Blazer as we walk.

"One I will keep for now, Mr. De Luca."

It's not customary for a Vigilante to refuse to introduce himself upon meeting a contemporary. Either they do things differently in this syndicate or he's been instructed not to give it. Troublesome.

I glance at Mia to gauge her level of concern. If she is with Jovana, she should be sweating bullets. Other than her discomfort with the shoes, though, she seems calm and curious. I'm bothered that I can't peg her classification.

I'm never fooled. So either Mia is not with Jovana, or once again she is surprising me with her competence. I will know soon enough.

We pass through the outer threshold and into a small holding chamber typical of silo entries. The heavy steel doors behind us slide closed, and the shiny ones ahead hiss open. Beyond is a hallway flanked by thick glass screens patterned with faint, embedded circuits. This is what I've waited for.

We'll be scanned and our information displayed as we pass.

"Step forward, please," Mr. Blazer says.

I can feel Mia hesitate, but I take her hand and lead her into the glass hall.

As soon as I step in, the panels on my side light up with information. My name. Vitals. Last known locations. The words "Ridley Prison" are highlighted at the bottom in bold red. Next to them flashes the word "Fugitive" like an accusation. Nothing unexpected, and I am pleased that no notice of the past twenty-four hours has registered. Not even Mia's safe house. The car is well cloaked. My identification has been hidden until now.

I glance over at the other side where Mia's information is displayed.

Or should be.

Instead of the wall of text like mine, Mia's is a blank slate. Only her name shows, nothing else. Impossible.

The Identipad records can have holes and hidden information, but the security scanner at a silo should show everything. Even if someone has been wiped, there's always minimal information. But it's like Mia doesn't exist beyond her name.

I mask my surprise, but Running Man completely fails to hide his.

"What the hell?" he says and gestures at Mia's wall of screens. "Jones, you seeing this?"

"Be quiet, fool," he snaps. "Yes, I see it."

I try to remember a Jones from my Vigilante days, but it's too common a name to be memorable.

Jones says nothing more but moves between me and Mia. "Please come with me," he says. He puts his hand on her shoulder and presses her forward.

I step in front of them. "Where are you taking her?"

"That's not your concern, pal," says Running Man. He moves in next to me, too close for my taste. My irritation is pricked.

"It is my concern, as she may have information pertinent to my situation." I fold my arms across my chest. The knife is still in my hand, but I make an effort not to flash it. An open threat would be a very bad idea right now.

Jones's face darkens. "Ms. Morrow has no information for fugitives."

I feel my anger rising and take a deep breath. "I am the former director of the West Coast syndicate. The only reason I'm here is to clear my name, and that girl may have information useful to that end."

Running Man sneers at me, inches from my face. "You're nothing now."

He doesn't even see it coming. With a quick twist of my body I slam the flat of my palm against his shoulder and hook my foot behind his leg. He spins and falls hard to the ground, limbs flailing. I'm right with him and drive my knee into his chest. He gasps and tries to suck in air. All cockiness is gone.

"Stand down!" booms a voice behind us.

I risk a glance and see a man in a suit striding down the hall. His eyes are dark, stern, and demand attention, if not respect. I rise to my feet with a fluid motion, careful to keep my hands at my sides and the knife in view. Running Man struggles up to his knees, still sucking in noisy breaths. Out of the corner of my eye I see Jones smirk and give a small shake of his head. So much for his hotshot bodyguard.

The new arrival stops several feet away, eyes moving from me, to Running Man, and finally to Mia. He studies her for a minute before shifting his gaze back to me.

"Jones, please take Ms. Morrow to the East Room. You, Mr. De Luca," he says and points at me, "come with me." He turns and strides back toward the doors at the end.

I don't follow. "I would prefer Ms. Morrow stay with me."

The man stops and turns around. "That's not possible at the moment. And I strongly advise you to come with me. Especially if you truly wish to clear your name."

Mia glances at me as Jones hurries her past. Confusion and concern rim her eyes, and I feel that pang in my chest. I almost reach out and grab her arm but check myself at the last second. I don't have many options at the moment, and they've made it clear that staying with Mia is not one of them.

16

MIA

I have to stuff down my panic at being separated from Jax. Funny how quickly your abductor becomes your only familiar face. I'm not sure if I'm going from frying pan straight to fire. Or if I'm saved.

Jones, the man in the brown blazer, guides me gently by the elbow as we go down a short hallway. I turn to look behind me for Jax, but he and the man in the suit are already gone from the glass corridor.

Jax's information still lights up the display, the word FUGITIVE pulsing red.

"This way, Ms. Morrow," Jones says.

"Where are you taking me?" I ask.

"Just to our visitor lounge." As we approach a set of steel doors, a scanner sends a green light across his body. The panels open for us.

We enter what seems to be an elevator, but there are no buttons.

The doors close, and we start going down. I reach for the wall to steady myself in the crazy shoes. Before I can even ask where we're going or how this elevator is controlled, the doors slide open again.

The corridor ahead is oval shaped, barely taller than us and only slightly wider. The walls are smooth and metal. Jones leads the way, and I try to walk more normally. I am determined to get the hang of these heels. I try not to think about what will happen if I have to try to escape in them.

"What is this place?" I ask.

"It's an old missile silo," Jones says pleasantly. He slows his pace to accommodate my unsteady gait.

"But what is it now?" I ask. "Those glass walls

we came through aren't from a missile silo."

We arrive at another set of doors. Again Jones is scanned. But before the steel panels can part, he holds up his hand, palm forward. A red light blinks and the doors stay closed. My anxiety rises.

"How much did Jax tell you?" he asks.

He's fishing for information. I don't want to get Jax in trouble.

"Nothing," I say innocently. "He says he found me at a safe house and therefore my identity was compromised. He thought I'd be safer here."

All lies. I can do this. I think of my mother, what she would say and do if she had no idea who was friend or enemy.

Jones nods. "Well, don't trouble yourself with any of that. We'll make sure your home is safe enough when we get you back."

My head snaps up. "I can go home?"

"Of course you can," he says. He lowers his hand and the light switches to green. The doors open smoothly.

For a moment, I can't connect what I see ahead of me with the bare metal tube we just walked through. It's like a hotel lobby. A few people wander through the plush space, artfully decorated with low sofas, a twisted metal sculpture in the center, and a long curving desk to one side.

At the desk, six women sit facing out, looking at a glass screen that separates them from the people passing by. Projected on the screen are images, words, maps, and dots. They busily move their hands over the information and talk into little microphones that come from their ears.

There is no natural light. The walls are marble but have no windows. We must be deep underground from the elevator ride.

A slender woman in a tailored pale blue suit approaches. "This must be Mia," she says and reaches for my hand. "You are surely exhausted. If I know Jax, he hasn't fed you or let you sleep."

"We slept — I slept," I say, fumbling for words.

Her expression doesn't change. "I'm Dell. I'll arrange for your return home." She nods at Jones. "I'll take it from here."

"It's been a pleasure," Jones says. Then he walks away. I feel abandoned again.

"How do you know Jax?" I ask.

The woman begins walking, and I assume I must follow.

"The question is, how do YOU?" she asks.

My suspicion is pricked. Does everyone here answer a question with a question? I decide to be stubborn. "I asked you first."

We cross the lobby and enter a carpeted hall. Dell smiles at me kindly. "I worked with Jax back on the West Coast," she says. "Six years of his crazy antics. There was this one time in Vegas with a bunch of MMA fighters having a brawl…" She trails off, shaking her head. "That Jax."

"Oh." I wonder now if maybe she and Jax had some sort of relationship. She's talking about him very familiarly. My stomach feels like lead. Dell is poised and beautiful and wears her heels with grace and ease. This is undoubtedly the sort of woman Jax is used to.

Not a naive country girl who can't handle her shoes.

I try to match her posture as I totter down the hall. I wonder what he is going through. Interrogation? Back to prison? He was so confident things would go well for him.

"Will I get to see Jax?" I ask.

Dell pauses by a tall steel door and waits to be scanned. "He's going to be in meetings today." Her tone is dismissive.

The handle pops open. "Let's get you something to eat while we arrange your transportation," she says.

I feel weird about just going home after everything that has happened. It seems so anticlimactic.

Dell leads me into what looks like a lounge. Curved sofas follow the rounded walls, all in subdued shades of gray and blue. Soft lamps give the room a peaceful glow. A long kidney-shaped coffee table is decorated with three small vases of bright pink flowers like exclamation marks in the calm space.

"Do you drink coffee? Tea?" Dell asks.

"Tea, thank you," I say. I sink onto one of the sofas and resist removing the uncomfortable shoes.

Dell sits a few cushions down. "I'm sure you've been quite lost and bewildered by all that's happened."

My concern pricks me again. What if they want to get information from me to use against Jax?

"So, when will I get to leave?" I ask.

Dell taps the face of what looks like an ordinary watch. On the wall, which appears to be glass over a light gray surface, an image appears. Dell skims the words, which mean nothing to me, just a string of Greek letters and coordinates and times.

"Surface time to your home in Tennessee is about six hours," she says. "But we have to get special dispensation to have transport brought in mid-shift." She smiles at me kindly. "But that will be no problem."

"Thank you for the trouble," I say uncertainly.

The door slides open and a young woman, maybe seventeen, enters the room with a tray. She is dressed oddly in a white pantsuit that looks like vinyl. "What an unusual outfit," I say.

"Katya is in training," Dell says. "This is her uniform."

Katya's chocolate eyes never leave me as she sets the tea set on the coffee table. "I've never met a special before," she says.

"That is all, Katya," Dell says sharply.

The girl's face flushes red. She turns and hurries out.

"What did she mean by 'special'?" I ask.

"Just someone outside our business interests being in the facility," Dell says. She pours a steaming cup of tea. "I hope Earl Grey is all right."

Suddenly I wonder if the tea is drugged. My heart pounds as Dell sets the pot back on the tray. "Sugar?" she asks. "Milk?"

I shake my head no. She moves the cup closer to me.

"Won't you have some?" I ask.

"Will that make you more comfortable?" She's on to me.

"Yes, I would like you to drink first." No sense hiding what I feel.

"Hanging with Jax would make anyone wary," Dell says. She pours another cup.

I screw up my courage and ask, "Did you and he…date?"

Dell laughs with a low throaty sound. "I wouldn't call it that."

I imagine the two of them entwined in bed.

I don't want to know any more. I pick up the cup, almost take a drink, then set it down again. Dell hasn't touched hers.

A small panel near the floor opens across the room, and a silver object rolls out like a metal bowling ball.

I resist the urge to pull my feet up on the sofa

as it travels across the carpet to rest by Dell's ankles.

"Ah, good," Dell says. She presses her palm to the surface of the ball. It glows green, and with a strange hiss, the top section pops up and twists open. Inside is a lovely bracelet with a line of clear crystals and a large gold clasp.

Dell picks it up. "Thank you," she says to the object, which responds by sealing itself closed and rolling back to the open panel.

Weird.

Dell turns to me. "This is a very important accessory for you," she says and slides closer to me. "It acts as a key to all the rooms in this building. You are free to move about this living space as well as a kitchen, bedroom, spa, and gym."

She snaps the bracelet on my wrist. "You are not a prisoner here, Mia. We want to get you home and back to your normal life. It's just not simple once you're brought to a facility as high security as this one."

I shake my wrist. The crystals tinkle together like any normal bracelet. "How does it work?"

"When the scanners get to it, the doors will just open for you."

"They don't know who I am, like the other people?"

Dell hesitates, as if weighing her words. "You are not in our system."

That makes sense. Everyone was so surprised that only my name popped up on those glass screens.

I glance around, realizing there are multiple identical door panels in the circular room. I'm no longer sure which one I came in.

"How do you get back aboveground?" I ask.

"Now that's another thing entirely," she says. "There are limited entry points. You'll be escorted for that."

"Will Jax do it?"

I see her patience is wearing thin on this subject. "I don't think you'll be seeing Mr. De Luca today."

Or ever again, if I understand her tone. I arrange my face into a simplistic smile and repeat my earlier question as though I'm not terribly sharp. "How long until I get to go?"

"As soon as we can arrange it."

Or, I think, as soon as I can get myself out of here and find Jax.

17

JAX

Two guards come through a side door to stand on either side of me.

One holds out his hand. "Knife, please," he says.

I hand it over. He drops it into a steel box. Again he holds out his hand.

"Holster and Blackphone, please."

I pull the phone out and pass it to him, making sure to press the secure lock button as I do. The phone gives a subtle vibration as confirmation. I expected they would take it, but I still lament the loss. Like Sam said, an untraceable blackout phone is a rare bird. I had hoped he had been able to rig a cloaking system, but obviously not.

"Holster," he repeats.

I reach inside my sleeve and snap it off.

"The ear mike, too," he says.

That stings a little. The small filament would have been useful even without the Blackphone. I carefully extract the mike from my ear and give it to him.

"Watch," he adds.

The watch disappears into the box.

The man in the suit steps forward. "That everything?" he asks the guards.

One of them nods. "All that we saw on the scanners," he says.

They missed the skeleton key, thankfully. It's ultra thin, and Sam must not have handed that particular tech over to the syndicate yet. I'm grateful to be one step ahead.

The suited man motions down a hallway. "Mr. De Luca, if you would be so kind as to come this way." He leads us down the corridor. One of the guards follows.

"So, why does a fugitive like yourself waltz up to our front door?" he asks.

"Testing your defenses, perhaps?" I ask.

"I assure you, Mr. De Luca, your approach was noted long before you arrived."

How much of that statement is true? I wonder. The data screens clearly showed they lost track of me after my escape from Ridley. Do they know the car is mine? Or is this man simply trying to throw me off guard?

I give him a grunt of acknowledgment. "So who are you, then?"

"Alan Carter, head of this syndicate."

"A contemporary of mine, then," I say, keeping my voice pleasant. "Can't say I ever made the trip out here before."

"Indeed." Carter's tone is haughty, tinged with suspicion. "It's been my experience that those on the coasts only talk to us when they want something."

"My needs are quite simple, I assure you."

He stops and studies my face for a moment. I give him a small yet warm smile.

"Are they now." It's a statement, not a

question. His eyes are cold.

Carter moves on, and the guard gives me a firm push to keep moving, as if I'm a common criminal. This does not bode well for how quickly I might be cleared of my charges.

We walk the hall in silence until we reach an actual silo that once housed a nuclear missile. A few vintage posters are framed and hang on the wall. "Ready to launch at a moment's notice!" reads one, sporting a rocket with a smiling face. Another shows a soldier holding a missile and says, "Defend our freedom from the Reds!"

I've been in similar silos in the old Soviet Union. It's amusing to see almost identical posters there, pointing to America as the bad guys.

Now the silo holds multiple floors with a central open atrium. On each floor are desks and glass screens displaying a dizzying array of information. I spot one collection of screens all tuned to different news broadcasts from the national outlets. Pop-ups appear frequently, pointing out locations and threat analyses of the information. Additional information scrolls along the bottom.

This is the nerve center, where the syndicate collates all the information coming in the countless feeds, sifting through it and parceling it out for later analysis. What I wouldn't give for a few minutes at one of the terminals to try to locate Klaus. Sam and Colette found nothing on their own, but they were limited by the necessity of avoiding any association with me. There would be so much more information here.

Carter has other ideas, though. He leads me down several levels and along another hallway before stopping at a door. A scanner runs a beam over Carter and the door opens. The three of us enter a spartan room with only a white table and two chairs. The plain walls enhance the harsh lighting. In the middle of the table is a small black dome. It is the only thing in the room that is not white.

Carter motions for me to sit in the chair on the far side of the table. He settles opposite me. A guard stands near the door, staring impassively. Occasionally his eyes flit between me and Carter.

I've been in interrogation rooms before, but not on this side of the table. I fold my hands on the cool surface and say nothing. Eventually Carter pulls out a tablet and scrolls through information. He frowns several times, then puts it down with a sigh. The screen winks out before I can see what it says.

"Trespassing, unauthorized access of syndicate systems, attempted bribery, assault and battery of a civilian police officer, and murder of a fellow Vigilante," he says. "Not to mention escape from an authorized penitentiary. How again were you thinking to prove your innocence when none of this is in dispute? Of which of these crimes do you claim innocence, Mr. De Luca?"

"None of them." I spread my hands. "They're all true." I hesitate. "Except the bribery. I was just paying a hooker."

Carter's eyes narrow. "This is not amusing. You don't seem to understand your position."

I put my hands on the desk and lean forward, staring hard at Carter. "I need to speak with Sutherland." Sutherland is the head of the American syndicate. He presides over all the regions, a position I was once in line to accept.

Carter doesn't bat an eye. "And why do you think Sutherland can help you?"

"Because," I say in a tone I might use with a child, "he has final arbitration over conflict between two Vigilantes. Ergo, he can clear my name." I straighten back up in the seat and resume my neutral posture.

Carter sighs, as if his job is too much for him today. "What if I told you Sutherland has already notified me that he does not want to speak with you?"

"Not possible—" I begin, but Carter cuts me off.

"He was alerted the moment we recognized your heat signature. Furthermore, he has instructed me to place you into custody until such time that you can be transferred to a maximum-security penitentiary, one where you can't simply walk out the front door."

An uncomfortable prickle creeps up my neck. I had not counted on Sutherland outright refusing to speak with me. This is not the Sutherland I know.

But then, neither is the one who would allow a syndicate director to rot in jail without a tribunal.

Still, I have to call the bluff.

"I would call you a liar, Mr. Carter," I say. "Sutherland is my mentor and personal friend."

Carter spins the tablet around and brings up the display. A picture of me appears along with the same basic vitals as in the glass entry hall. However, beneath the word "fugitive" is a new sentence.

By order of Director Sutherland, former operative Jax De Luca is ordered held for transfer to New Attica Correctional Facility upon apprehension.

That prickle becomes a full-on spear to my head. This is not possible. Ever since the police rebellion four years ago, New Attica has been one of the worst prisons in the country.

For Sutherland to order my incarceration in that hellhole is serious.

I keep my discomfort buried deep and focus on feeling every part of my body. The concentration rapidly calms me and I allow myself a steady, even breath before giving Carter a small smile. I reach out and spin the pad back to him.

"It says nothing about asking questions," I say.

Carter shrugs. "Go ahead. I won't guarantee answers you like. Or answers at all."

I decide to be direct. "Where is Operative Klaus?"

Carter gives me a puzzled look, so I press on. "Klaus. He was with the German syndicate before transferring to America years ago. He was my partner, but now he has vanished. I fear his security has been compromised and his life may be in danger."

Carter picks up the tablet and taps on it. He frowns after a few seconds. "I don't see a record for an Operative Klaus."

Another unpleasant surprise. "Are you spelling it correctly? His last known location was the Tennessee safe house."

"No," Carter says. "There's nothing."

"Vigilantes don't just vanish!" I growl. "He has an entry in the system! I know because I entered the details myself as syndicate director!"

Carter eyes me coldly, his mouth a tight line. "Perhaps this was the 'unauthorized access of syndicate systems' I noted earlier?"

My calm snaps. I shoot up out of my chair and send it flying back with a clatter. The guard leaps forward, a Taser in his hand. I hold my ground behind the desk, fuming. I can feel my anger flowing off me in heated waves, but tamp it down enough to keep my voice steady.

"Klaus was my friend," I say through gritted teeth. "He had an entry. When a record is deleted, the system is flagged." I lean over the table. "Search. The. Flags."

Carter stares at me a moment, and I think he'll just deny my request. But he picks up the tablet. As he taps, concern crosses his brow and his finger strikes on the surface become faster, more insistent.

"All right," he says. "I found a flag in the system attached to the name Klaus. It's not a personnel record. Just a death notice."

"A what?" I lean closer.

"It's weird." Carter keeps tapping. "If I search the flags, I show a death notice for Klaus, but no evidence that he was ever alive."

"How did he die?" My throat is tight.

"It doesn't say. Just that he's dead." Carter frowns. "This is high-level tampering. Nobody can die without having a living record."

"May I?" I hold out my hand for the tablet.

Carter hesitates, then hands it over. I quickly search for flags on deleted entries involving the Tennessee safe house.

Sure enough, one comes up. The closure of the safe house due to "toxic chemical contamination." It's the same date and entry as Klaus's death.

There is no toxic chemical there. It was a ploy to close it. To hide what they did.

Klaus died at the safe house and someone

deleted him to cover their tracks.

Jovana.

And her lackey temptress.

Mia.

I push the pad at Carter and sit back down.

But Carter stands to leave. "I'll be sure to add this to my report," he says. "Perhaps your role in helping identify the fraudulent record will be of help to you in a future hearing." He shrugs. "If you survive even a day in New Attica."

He nods at the guard and the two of them move to the door.

It hisses closed behind them.

I'm alone for the moment, but I'm not done here. I still have a skeleton key.

And I have a lying, murdering honey-haired safe house operative to locate in this building. And to interrogate. And if necessary, to take out of commission.

18

MIA

I'm sick of sitting with this Dell woman. I want out of here to find Jax.

The doors open again, and the girl Katya enters with a tray of small sandwiches.

Dell stands up. "Katya, you sit with Mia a while. I'm going to check on the status of her release approval."

Katya nods as she sets the tray on the coffee table. She perches uncertainly on the far end of the sofa.

Dell turns to me. "I'll be back very shortly. Let us know if you need anything to make you comfortable."

I glance down at the stilettos. "You wouldn't happen to have a shoe store nearby, would you?"

Not that I have money. I left home with only a now-destroyed nightgown and my Crocs. Not so much as a driver's license, I realize. No one would know if I disappeared. No one would even look, other than maybe the neighbor, Shirley.

"You'll be home soon," Dell says. "We're here to help you."

She exits through the door. To keep track of which one she uses, I imagine I am sitting at six o'clock and the door is at two. Maybe I can keep them straight that way. Katya came in at ten o'clock, so the kitchen must be that way.

"Are you hungry?" Katya asks.

She has straight blond hair that just touches her shoulders. She's pretty and fresh looking, no makeup, just the white pantsuit. I glance at her feet in white sneakers. I could use a pair of those. They look about my size.

I realize Dell never drank her tea. "A little

hungry," I say. "But I have a rule never to drink alone." I push Dell's cup toward Katya. "Dell poured this but didn't drink any."

Katya stares at the cup with undisguised concern. She's not very good at hiding her thoughts, at least not yet. Jax would eat her alive. Now I feel sure the tea is drugged. I wonder how to get out of here.

But she picks up the cup and takes a sip. I watch her a moment, wondering if she is just not aware of what they have done.

Although I guess she probably *made* the tea.

When several minutes pass in awkward silence and nothing happens to her, I dump three spoonfuls of sugar in the cup and drink it greedily. I'm starving and thirsty and need calories if I'm going to escape this place. I don't know if they told the truth about the bracelet or if it just tracks me. For all I know it'll stick me with poison the minute I try to go anywhere.

"So why did you call me special?" I ask Katya, when I figure she's at her most uncomfortable due to the silence and her awkward position on the sofa.

"Because you are one," she says quietly.

"How did you know just by looking?"

"You have a zero screen," she says.

"A what?"

She points above my head. "A zero screen. You can't see them? They are angled to be visible only for your direct view." She scoots down the sofa and reaches for my bracelet. "Twist this one." She turns a crystal on its gold hoop.

Above her, on the glass screen, appears a set of data like the one when Jax and I entered the facility.

Katya Reynolds. Age 18. Phase One Trainee.

Hey. That's what Jax kept calling ME.

"What's a Phase One Trainee?" I ask.

"It's the status of anyone in their first year of training," she says. "Why don't you know that?" Her eyes get wide, like she's just screwed up.

"I've been in a safe house," I say. Maybe I can fake this. "For my protection."

"You're not much older than me," she says. "You don't seem like you'd be a special."

"Is that why I don't have one of those over my head?" I say, gesturing toward her wall screen.

"You do. Yours is just blank except for your name. That makes you a special," she says.

I turn around to see my screen. Sure enough, all it says is "Mia Morrow," the same as when we walked in the glass hall.

"But Dell said I just wasn't in the system."

"Everybody's in the system," Katya says. "From the moment your mother gets a positive pregnancy test."

I shudder at the thought of someone watching a woman peeing on a stick.

It's time to figure out where I am and what I'm doing here, before Dell comes back. Katya is infinitely easier to manipulate.

I pick up a sandwich and take a big bite as I think about what to say to Katya. I wonder if our conversation is being monitored. Of course it is.

My neck itches where Jax put that sedative device and I press my hand to it. "This is so annoying," I say. She knew about the bracelet. Maybe she can deactivate this. "Do you know how to remove it?"

"It's just a tracker," she says. "You can pull it off."

Obviously she doesn't know what it is. "It will sedate me if I do," I say.

"No," she argues. "That's definitely one of the first things we learn to identify. It's just a tracker." She reaches out for me.

I try to smack her arm away, but when I connect, I realize Katya is a lot more than she seems. Her arm is like steel. What we can't see beneath that generic white suit is a solid layer of muscle.

I feel a sharp tug against my skin.

"It's best to yank it like a Band-Aid," she says. "See?" She has the device in her palm.

I slap my hand against my neck, already feeling woozy. I sag against the sofa.

Katya turns the adhesive strip over. "Just a GPS model. An old one. No sedative."

I stare at it. There's nothing but a fine wire curled inside.

I sit up. She's right. I'm fine.

Then I'm mad.

Ohhhh, that Jax. I could have run at any time! I burn with rage. He thought I was so stupid.

Katya sets the adhesive strip on the table. "How long were you in that safe house? This is a really old device. It should have been in your training even if it was years ago."

A yellow bar on the wall catches my eye. It's Katya's screen. There's now an extra icon at the bottom. It blinks steadily. I have a funny feeling it has to do with our conversation, and that Dell will come back any second to keep me from finding out anything else.

No more sitting around this place, whatever it is. I want to get the layout, make a plan. I stand and head to the door at ten o'clock, the one Katya came through. "Does this go to the kitchen?"

Katya jumps up. "Yes. You want to see the place?" She seems relieved to do something other than talk.

"Yes," I say. "Let's do that."

When I approach the door, the scanner begins its journey, then stops at the bracelet. The doors open instantly.

Excellent. Maybe I am a little bit special.

Now to figure out how to steal this girl's shoes.

19

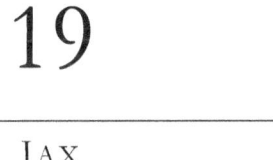

JAX

The interrogation room is silent and chilly. I stare at the black dome on the table. Inside are cameras, microphones, and thermal sensors. Everything that just happened will be stored in my file for future reference.

I'll give them an eyeful when I find Mia. Just picturing her makes me hot with rage.

She'll tell me what happened to Klaus. I will hold nothing back now that I know he died in her safe house. Vigilantes are authorized to use any force necessary against civilians.

I know I'm being watched via the dome, so I make sure I appear calm and composed until I strike.

The doors work on scanner technology, probably keyed to heat signatures, DNA if they are the latest models. This means I will have to act fast to get one open before it scans me and sets off an alarm. It also means most personnel here won't think twice about someone wandering the halls, since the scanners keep unauthorized personnel corralled.

Even so, I'll have limited time once I leave this room to find Mia. I need them to think I'm still in here. The skeleton key can probably cloak my position for a few seconds, but that will not do me much good with a camera visual. Unless…

I slowly, carefully, slip the thin bit of cellophane out of its hidden pocket. I pop it on the underside of the table and set it to analyzing the nonexistent lock to confuse it.

I take off my jacket. The key beeps in error because it's not attached to a locking mechanism, but that's not what I'm after. A quick tap sets the key to power surge. The dome crackles with static from the unexpected jolt.

I toss my jacket over the dome and retrieve the key. If I've done this correctly, it will seem as if the camera simply malfunctioned and shut down. They'll send someone to check, but I'll have several minutes before a technician arrives.

Hopefully. I don't intend to stick around to find out.

I step to the door and put the key against it, near the frame. The scanner begins its journey down my body, but I quickly tap a command. A second later it beeps, and the scan stops. The door pops open. I release my held breath. Sam is a genius.

The hallway beyond is empty. I pull the key off the door and walk back toward the central silo. If I guessed right about their security protocol, no one there will pay me any mind as long as I don't draw undue attention to myself. Time to test that theory.

I enter the central silo and pause for a quick glance, looking for an unoccupied station. I spot one on the next level up, across from where I am. Staying close to the wall, I circle the silo and head up the stairway. At the top I stand aside to let someone pass by on the stairs. He looks at me with a blank expression and I give him a polite nod.

"Pardon me," he says, and continues on his way down.

I breathe a sigh of relief. Another test passed. As long as I don't encounter anyone who actually knows me, I'll be fine. None of the hallways have glass screens that will give away my name or fugitive status as I walk. The rooms are another matter, but I don't plan to enter any.

I arrive at the empty terminal. The interface is familiar, and I pull up a map of the complex. Nothing is labeled, but it looks like the entire east wing is an addition to the original military installation. Carter said Mia was going to the "East Room." She's probably somewhere in that addition, but where?

The tracker.

I told Mia the sticker on her neck was capable of all sorts of tricks, but really it's nothing more than a GPS locator, seriously old tech. If I still had my Blackphone this would be child's play, but even without it I can find her if the system here is set up like the ones on the West Coast. I tap through a few screens. Tracking a person would require a log-in that would compromise my identity. But I'm just doing an inventory check on the devices, same as any low-level worker could do.

Bingo. The screen lights up, showing the location of trackers in the complex. A cluster of them are together far below, probably a storage room. But one is all by itself. In the east wing.

Mia.

I memorize the layout of the complex. We can't go out the front door, obviously, but there are six emergency hatches. Four of them have scanners for access and actual guards. Two are in an unused section of the silo. Probably permanently sealed. I can probably take out the guards, although it's risky with Mia in tow. I may have to take a chance on the others.

Between Mia and the unused hatches are a number of those scanner doors, but I should be able to pop them open with the skeleton key. Until they figure out I'm gone and put the whole silo on lockdown.

No time to waste.

I set the terminal back to what it displayed when I found it. Another trip up the stairs takes me down a connecting passage to a second missile silo. Unlike the one I just left, this silo is still bare concrete, just a huge circle that once housed the actual missile.

Below me sits a helicopter at the ready. Too bad that thing would light up like a Christmas tree on every Vigilante sensor if I flew it out of here. It would be a great means of escape otherwise.

No, on foot is the only way. I will take pleasure dragging Mia through the woods in her ankle-breaking shoes. Nothing will be too harsh for that murdering liar.

Down the corridor to the east wing, I pass two young women in Phase One white suits. We exchange pleasantries as we pass. I try to picture Mia in one of their outfits, but it's no use. She was never a Vigilante. She's the enemy.

At the entrance to the east wing is one of the scanner doors. I think this one will be as simple as the one to the interrogation room.

But this one starts scanning me several feet away, costing me precious seconds. I slap the key on the frame. The green line sweeps down as the key's display lights up and flashes different codes. A second crawls by. The beam is below my waist. I'm not sure what will happen if it IDs me. If we go into lockdown, I'm screwed.

Just as the beam hits my knees, the key beeps and the beam vanishes. The door slides open. I grab the key from the frame and say a silent thanks that it got me through another door.

But this journey is taking too long. I sense my time is about up.

I hurry down another hallway, this one much more modern than the others and decorated in soft blues and grays. Another turn and the room should be straight ahead. No one else is in this wing, at least so far. That's a good thing, because every inch of the place has glass on the walls. My info screen is displayed for anyone who will pass by. The pulsing red of the fugitive label is visible at a good distance.

Obviously, unauthorized guests are regular visitors to this section of the silo. Quite possibly the system has already sent out a silent alarm. When I was director, my silo did not have a wing like this, so I do not know the protocol.

Mia's room should be dead ahead. Yes, I see it. It has a window looking in. Probably a one-way mirror. I approach it carefully.

Mia passes in front of the window and my stride falters. I am so angry at her. I know she had a hand in killing Klaus. But now that I see her again, I remember how innocent she looks. How lost.

I stuff it down. She is the enemy.

Just as I walk up to the door, an alarm goes off. Damn it. Mia looks around at the noise.

I slap the key on the door. The display lights up and scans through the codes, then gives me a discouraging noise. I reset it and try again.

Nothing. The door won't open. Lockdown. Shit.

The one-way mirror. Can I break it? I have nothing to protect my hand, so I rear back and give the window a solid side kick. It vibrates but otherwise doesn't budge. Mia looks at it, startled. She backs away.

"Mia!" I shout. She doesn't react to my voice, but stares at the mirror from her side. I kick it again and she jumps back. The window holds.

I look around, pushing the panic down and taking deep, calming breaths. There must be something nearby I can use to smash this window open. Nothing. The hall is empty.

I hear a door open and whirl at the sound, expecting a horde of Vigilantes barreling down on me.

"Jax?"

Mia stands in the open doorway.

"Jax," she says again, "what are you doing?"

My mind snaps back to attention. She can't think I'm on to her, or she won't come with me.

"We've got to get out of here," I say. Without waiting for her response, I grab her hand and pull her back down the hallway. She comes willingly. She's somehow traded her high heels for a pair of Phase One Trainee uniform shoes, so we take off at a run.

Once I have her out of this silo, she's going to pay for what she's done.

20

Mia

Thank God I got the shoes off Katya. I can't wait to tell Jax how. He'll be so proud of me, I think. Maybe it'll prove I'm worthy of staying with him.

Jax drags me down the hall at a breakneck pace. We approach another door and he sticks a bit of tape to it, or something, then pounds on the steel when it refuses to open. I lift my bracelet and the panels smoothly slide apart.

He stares at me a moment, dumbfounded. "That shouldn't work during a lockdown."

I give a little shrug. "I'm special."

Jax takes his tape again and we head down another hallway, this one unfinished with bare concrete.

We come to another door, older, with an actual handle. There is no scanning device above it. I shake my bracelet at it, but nothing happens.

Jax grins. "We're not in Kansas anymore."

I have no idea what he means, but he turns and delivers three swift kicks to the handle. The metal groans and dents in.

He braces both hands on the lever and jerks it swiftly down. Something snaps inside, and the door opens.

"Low tech," he says.

The lights are dim in this hall, and I can hear the drip of water.

"This way," Jax says. We run along the concrete walls until we come to a rusting ladder. He glances down at my shoes. "Lucky break."

I want to tell him luck had nothing to do with it, but he's already halfway up the ladder. It disappears into a dark circular space. I'm hesitant to follow.

"Come on," he calls down. "Don't make me come for you."

I hear a crashing sound down the hall and figure they're on to our location even without their fancy gadgets. I stick my foot on the bottom rung and heave myself up.

The tunnel we're climbing is dank and musty smelling. Jax is waiting a few feet up. "Don't get us caught," he hisses.

"Just cloak us or something," I hiss back.

"We're escaping the old-fashioned way," he says and starts climbing again.

"So they took your toys," I say.

"Something like that."

Once we've climbed a little way, it's fully dark. "How are you even going to see to get out of here?" I ask. I'm not loving trying to feel my way in the pitch black on a slippery ladder with a long fall if I miss.

My hand brushes against his shoe. He's stopped.

"They can shoot up this ladder, you know," I whisper.

"We're at the hatch," he says.

He moves around a little, then I see a strange rectangle of light with a few images on it. It's his sticky tape he's been putting on all the doors. I guess he got to keep one toy.

"Go back down about six rungs," he says.

Going down is way worse than going up. I fish around with my foot to find each bar, terrified I will lose my grip.

"Any day now," he says, his voice low and angry.

Above us, an electrical flash momentarily blinds me.

"What was that?" I squeal.

"Trying to break the latch seal," he says. I hear his shoes clanging on the metal as he goes back to the top. The device still emits a bit of light, enough to see shadows.

Jax grunts, pushing up on the hatch. After a moment, a rim of light appears around the edge, then it widens.

I see sky.

"Oh, my God!" I say. "We're out!"

"Take care," Jax says. "They may be ready for us."

I clutch at the ladder. I'm so glad I'm away from those people and back with Jax, I could cry.

Jax crouches on the ladder, then springs up and out in one powerful movement, like a lion.

I pause, waiting for the sounds of fighting or gunfire. Nothing.

He peers back down. "Come on. We're clear, but they have our heat signatures again, so they'll be here any minute."

I hurry up the ladder. The feel of dirt and rocks beneath my fingers as I stumble out is amazing. We're back in the woods. I want to kiss the ground.

"They can't get a visual in the trees, so keep moving." Jax grips my arm as we race ahead.

"But they can follow our heat," I say.

Jax races toward a huge boulder. I don't know why he's dragging me that way. It's wide open, without any trees to hide us.

"Not for long," he says. Without warning, he scoops me into his arms and races across the stone surface.

Then we're falling.

I clutch at him. The air is cold on my face as we hurtle down. I try to open my eyes and look at him. What has he done?

Then we're underwater.

I break away, fighting for the surface in my heavy sweater dress. I'm dragged down by the weight of it. I haven't been swimming in years, not since my parents died. After their boating accident, I didn't go into the water anymore. I thrash around, panicked.

Strong arms come around me.

My face bobs above the water. Jax holds me against his chest, kicking us closer to the shore, working with the current.

"You should learn to swim," he says.

"You should ask before throwing women off cliffs," I snap back.

"We need to stay in the water as long as possible," he says.

"Do you even know where the car is from here?" I ask.

"Of course I do."

We float along another minute. I try to catch my breath. Above us, the sky is bright blue. Birds flit over the river, as if the people below them are simply going for a swim after a romantic picnic.

I'm freezing, my teeth chattering, and the dress is so heavy I almost want to take it off.

"Nearly there," Jax says.

He guides us toward the riverbank.

I pull away from him. "I can swim," I say. "Just not when I'm surprised."

"Doesn't matter now."

I understand what he means when my feet hit bottom. The edge of the river is littered with leaves and bramble. I fight my way through it to get to solid ground.

Jax stops me with his hands.

"We should stay cold enough to escape detection as we get to the car, but they may have already confiscated it. Be prepared to be captured. I have no communication devices. We're out here on our own skills." His blue-gray eyes pierce mine. "If you have any special training, now would be a good time to tell me what you can do."

I don't know what to say. "I can make sailing knots."

His face flickers for a moment with some unreadable emotion. "Fine. We'll see how it goes."

He takes off at a loose run.

I grab the dripping base of my skirt and hitch it up over my knees so I can keep up. "We'll see how it goes?" I ask. "That's all you've got? The big tough Vigilante with all those fancy gadgets?"

"That's all I've got," he says, his voice cold.

I want to jump on his back and pummel him, but the situation is too dire. If they take us back to the silo, what then? Will I still be special? Or a fugitive like him? The crystals still tinkle on my wrist.

Jax hears them and halts. "Damn it," he says. He snatches the bracelet and splits it apart. The crystals fall all over the leaves.

Of course. They can track me with it.

He takes off at a sprint now and it's all I can do to keep him in sight ahead of me. When I think I can't go another step, I see the car ahead. Thank God.

Except, the tire is still flat.

Jax stands by a tree off to one side.

I come up next to him, sucking in air. "They took your keys, didn't they?"

"I'm not that foolish." He emits a high-pitched whistle.

"Do they come when you call them?" I ask.

The key chain falls from the tree neatly into his hand. "Something like that," he says. "Now get in."

I wrench open the passenger door.

Jax jumps inside and has the car in motion before I can pull the handle closed. All his dash monitors are issuing warning beeps. The grid with the dots pulses red in every direction.

"Have they found us?" I ask.

"They're about to."

Jax slams on the gas and drives us out of the trees. We hit the gravel in a full skid. He yanks on the wheel and we head to the highway.

"They're totally going to follow us," I say.

"Yes, they are," he says.

"But you have a plan?" I ask.

"Of course," he says.

Now that we're in the car, I feel a crazy sense of elation. I can't help it, but let out a little squeal.

"What?" Jax asks.

"This is so exciting!"

I've never been so crazy hyper before. I don't care anymore how I got into this world, that Jax tied me up and dragged me into it. It feels right. I belong here. This is the best I've ever felt in my life.

"They were going to send me home," I tell Jax. "Like I could go back there after all this!"

Jax careens down the road. The red blips concentrate on a spot well behind us. I'm betting that's where my bracelet is. I squeal again. We fooled them!

"Would you stop with that damn noise?" Jax growls.

"I'm too excited!" I punch him on the arm. "What are we doing next? Where are we going? Did you find out where Klaus is? I want to meet him!"

With that, Jax jerks off the road and we're back in the woods again.

21

JAX

I'm not sure what game Mia is playing, but I'm done going along.

I grab her by the neck and squeeze a spot that I know creates a screaming pain through her skull.

Her eyes go bright with pain, but she can't easily speak while I'm doing this.

My voice is like ice. "Who killed Klaus? Was it you? Or Jovana? Or one of her people?"

I let go. She slumps forward so fast that her

forehead bangs the dash.

I wait until I know she is recovered enough to hear me. "Who killed Klaus?" I ask again.

Her back shakes a little, and that annoying protective urge in me is pricked again. I ignore it. "Answer me," I insist, "or I'll do that again."

She sucks in a long shuddering breath. "I—I thought I was special," she manages to get out.

I grab her shoulder and drag her back against her seat. "I am aware that you have somehow managed to compromise the Vigilante information network. That is no small feat." I pull my hand away. "That doesn't tell me who killed Klaus."

She turns her face to me, eyes wet with pain and fear. "Klaus is dead?"

If her training is this good, I need to know who did it, because her confusion, fear, and innocence are so convincing that I let go of her and sit back.

"He was killed at your safe house, six months ago. Both his record and the notification of his death were deleted."

She shakes her head. "No. I was there with my aunt. That's right when I arrived. Almost to the day." Her eyes plead with me. "We were alone. Nobody was killed there. I never heard of the

Vigilantes until you told me."

I want to tear out my hair, a feeling I'm not used to. Interrogating difficult prisoners was something I used to do all the time. Why is this pathetic sniveling girl getting to me?

I reach to tap my watch, realize it was confiscated at the silo, and manually bring up the dash screen. "Encrypted message," I say.

The display flashes red, then green. "Encryption initiated," it says.

"Message to Sam and Colette. Klaus dead. Records deleted. Rendezvous in—" I glance at the countdown to when I have to give up the ID of the car. I can't push it. "Thirty-six hours." I give a set of coordinates that will put us near the safe house.

Mia sniffs. "They were going to send me home." She rubs her neck. "But I didn't want to go."

I cut off the communication screen so that it won't add her ramblings to my message. Her voice sounds so forlorn, so lost.

"All right, I'll play," I say. "Why didn't you want to go home?"

Her green eyes search mine. She looks me over, my hair, the white shirt, now wet and sticking to me, my suit jacket still at the silo. They rest on my hand, which just caused her no small amount of pain.

"Because I want to be with you," she says. "All the way. With you."

22

MIA

There, I've said it.

Jax's expression is unreadable. I've just bared my pathetic heart. That I want him. I want this life. I don't want to go home. That he can tie me up. He can do anything he wants. I'm willing.

"Well?" I manage to ask.

The soft dings of the alarms suddenly increase in volume and speed.

Jax glances at the dash. "They've found us," he

says. "Damn it."

He wrenches open his door and dashes around to the trunk. I can't see what he's doing with it open, so I climb out of the car, tangled in the heavy, cold, wet dress.

When I get around to the back, Jax is pulling a large gelatinous brick from the trunk. Attached to it is a circuit board with a blinking green light.

"Time to give you your life back," he says to the brick and heaves it into the underbrush.

He slams the trunk.

"Well?" I ask again. "Will you keep me? I'll do anything you say. Anything you want."

He pauses for a second.

"You really have nothing to do with Jovana, do you?" he asks.

"No," I say. "I don't." My heart accelerates. I think he might be agreeing.

"And you're not trained in any way as an operative?"

"I have the shoes now," I say, lifting my foot in the white sneaker. "I can start."

He closes his eyes for a moment, and when they open again, they are glittering and hard.

"I can't have an innocent civilian come with

me," he says. "I'm a fugitive. I'm already putting my comrades in danger."

I take two steps closer to him. "Don't send me back to Tennessee. That's not where I belong. I can feel it."

Jax shakes his head. "We're done here. The Vigilantes obviously know you are a civilian. I'm not sure why they are protecting you, and it doesn't matter." He points into the woods where he threw the brick.

"You stay close to that, and they'll come for you. They'll take you home."

I lunge for him. "But I don't want to go home! I don't have a home! I have no one!"

I'm not going to let him go. I can't.

He hesitates a second, and my hope surges. He's changing his mind. He'll let me come with him.

"You have no choice, Mia," he says and pushes me away. "This is not the life for you." He heads around to his door.

I won't accept that.

I have to do something. He'll drive away, and then I'll never find him again.

He gets in the car and is about to pull the door

closed when I leap for it, blocking it with my body.

"Mia, step away," he says.

I've never done anything like what I'm about to do. I don't even know how. But I know Jax feels something for me. I have to show him that we're supposed to do this together, that he found me for a reason.

I'll seduce him. I'll be the persuasive woman that I was in my letters.

The letters. I glance behind Jax into the backseat. The red bondage rope is still strewn all over it from where I dug through my bag.

Without any hesitation, I jerk my sweater dress up to my waist to give my legs room to move. Jax looks down in surprise at the exposed red thong.

I throw a leg over him and straddle his body. I reach around him, far enough to grab the rope.

Then I'm back.

Jax puts his hands on my waist to lift me away. This gives me the perfect opportunity to wrap his arms in the rope and tie the fastest slipknot ever made. Before he can protest, I've got his arms over his head, four more knots locking him to the headrest. His elbows frame his face.

"Nicely done," he says bitterly. "You want the

Vigilantes to catch me, then?"

I swallow hard. I can hear the beeping of the alarm. I ignore it. I have faith that Jax can get us out of any jam.

I put my hands on his cheeks. His stubble isn't rough, like I thought, but soft. It cushions my palms.

His eyes are dark, a stormy gray-blue. I look at his lips. I'm going to have them. Twice he almost kissed me, but didn't. This time, I'm not going to let him get away.

I lean in, and we connect. His mouth is warm and softer than I expected. At first he just sits there and lets me move over his lips. I remember the bulge of him between us at the hotel, and I grind against his body.

His chest stills, and I know he's feeling this. His face relaxes beneath my hands. Now his mouth moves across mine, and he's kissing me instead of the other way around. His tongue slides between my lips and I automatically open.

I tilt my head to take him in as deeply as I can and a small groan escapes from my throat. I don't feel cold anymore, not at all, and heat blasts through my body as I move against him. He maneuvers away from my mouth, his lips on my jaw, my neck.

I'm utterly lost, drowning in his attention, fire licking through me everywhere we touch.

The ropes fall into our laps and I realize he's worked himself free. I want to laugh, thinking my silly knots could hold someone like Jax. His arms come around me and press me hard against him. Our mouths find each other again and I want to scream about this feeling I have as we dive into each other again.

His hands stroke my back, my ribs, and come down to my bared thighs. He spreads me wider so I can feel him, hard and erect, pushing up against me. I don't want anything between us. I want out of this heavy dress, to see him, to feel his skin.

The entire car lights up red inside. "Perimeter surrounded," the car voice says. "Security breach complete in fifteen seconds." It begins a countdown.

Jax breaks the kiss. "I hope this is what you wanted," he says. "Because we're about to get caught."

You've reached the end of Vigilante's Lover #1!

Eek! The endings are brutal! But we release fast!

Come ~~scream~~ talk about the cliffhangers
on Facebook with Annie's Vigilantes:

www.facebook.com/groups/anniesvigilantes

Join the mail list to make sure
you don't miss a release!

www.anniewinters.com

Annie has continued her grand tradition of killer
endings that began with her work as JJ Knight. Fans
don't call her the Queen of Cliffhangers for nothing!

Annie and Tony are modeling *Vigilante* after the
structure of television suspense series. We release
very quickly so you don't have long to wait!